A Man
And His Money

Frederic Stewart Isham

1st WORLD
LIBRARY
Literary Society

A Man and His Money

Frederic Stewart Isham

© 1st World Library – Literary Society, 2004
PO Box 2211
Fairfield, IA 52556
www.1stworldlibrary.org
First Edition

LCCN: 2005901322

Softcover ISBN: 1-4218-1137-5
Hardcover ISBN: 1-4218-1037-9
eBook ISBN: 1-4218-1237-1

Purchase *"A Man and His Money"*
as a traditional bound book at:
www.1stWorldLibrary.org/purchase.asp?ISBN=1-4218-1137-5

1st World Library Literary Society is a nonprofit
organization dedicated to promoting literacy by:

- Creating a free internet library accessible from any
computer worldwide.
- Hosting writing competitions and offering book
publishing scholarships.

A Man and His Money
contributed by Tim, Ed & Rodney
in support of
1st World Library Literary Society

CHAPTER I

THE COACH OF CONCORD

"Well? What can I do for you?"

The speaker - a scrubby little man - wheeled in the rickety office chair to regard some one hesitating on his threshold. The tones were not agreeable; the proprietor of the diminutive, run-down establishment, "The St. Cecilia Music Emporium," was not, for certain well defined reasons, in an amiable mood that morning. He had been about to reach down for a little brown jug which reposed on the spot usually allotted to the waste paper basket when the shadow of the new-comer fell obtrusively, not to say offensively, upon him.

It was not a reassuring shadow; it seemed to spring from an indeterminate personality. Mr. Kerry Mackintosh repeated his question more bruskly; the shadow (obviously not a customer, - no one ever sought Mr. Mackintosh's wares!) started; his face showed signs of a vacillating purpose.

"A mistake! Beg pardon!" he murmured with exquisite politeness and began to back out, when a somewhat brutal command on the other's part to "shut that d - door d - quick, and not let any more d - hot air out" arrested the visitor's purpose. Instead of retreating, he advanced.

"I beg pardon, were you addressing me?" he asked. The half apologetic look had quite vanished.

The other considered, muttered at length in an aggrieved tone something about hot air escaping and coal six dollars a ton, and ended with: "What do you want?"

"Work." The visitor's tone relapsed; it was now conspicuous for its want of "success waves"; it seemed to imply a definite cognizance of personal uselessness. He who had brightened a moment before now spoke like an automaton. Mr. Mackintosh looked at him and his shabby garments. He had a contempt for shabby garments - on others!

"Good day!" he said curtly.

But instead of going, the person coolly sat down. The proprietor of the little shop glanced toward the door and half started from his chair. Whereupon the visitor smiled; he had a charming smile in these moments of calm equipoise, it gave one an impression of potential possibilities. Mr. Mackintosh sank back into his chair.

"Too great a waste of energy!" he murmured, and having thus defined his attitude, turned to a "proof" of new rag-time. This he surveyed discontentedly; struck out a note here, jabbed in another there. The stranger watched him at first casually. By sundry signs the caller's fine resolution and assurance seemed slowly oozing from him; perhaps he began to have doubts as to the correctness of his position, thus to storm a man in his own castle, or office - even if it were such a disreputable-appearing office!

He shifted his feet thoughtfully; a thin lock of dark hair drooped more uncertainly over his brow; he got up. The composer dashed a blithe flourish to the tail of a note.

"Hold on," he said. "What's your hurry?" Sarcastically.

"Didn't know I was in a hurry!" There was no attempted levity in his tone, - he spoke rather listlessly, as one who had found the world, or its problems, slightly wearisome. The composer-publisher now arose; a new thought had suddenly assailed him.

"You say you are looking for work. Why did you drift in here?"

"The place looked small. Those big places have no end of applicants -"

"Shouldn't think that would phase you. With *your* nerve!"

The visitor flushed. "I seem to have made rather a mess of it," he confessed. "I usually do. Good day."

"A moment!" said Mr. Mackintosh. "One of my men" - he emphasized "one," as if their number were legion - "disappointed me this morning. I expect he's in the lockup by this time. Have you got a voice?"

"A what?"

"Can you sing?"

"I really don't know; haven't ever tried, since" - a wonderful retrospection in his tones - "since I was a little chap in church and wore white robes."

"Huh!" ejaculated the proprietor of the Saint Cecilia shop. "Mama's angel boy! That must have been a long time ago." The visitor did not answer; he pushed back uncertainly the uncertain lock of dark hair and seemed almost to have forgotten the object of his visit.

"Now see here" - Mr. Mackintosh's voice became purposeful, energetic; he seated himself before a piano that looked as if it had led a hard nomadic existence. "Now see here!" Striking a few chords. "Suppose you try this stunt! *What's the Matter with Mother*? My own composition! Kerry Mackintosh at his best! Now twitter away, if you've any of that angel voice left!"

The piano rattled; the new-comer, with a certain faint whimsical smile as if he appreciated the humor of his position, did "twitter away"; loud sounds filled the place. Quality might be lacking but of quantity there was a-plenty.

"Bully!" cried Mr. Mackintosh enthusiastically. "That'll start the tears rolling. *What's the Matter with Mother*? Nothing's the matter with mother. And if any one says there is - Will it go? With that voice?" He clapped his hand on the other's shoulder. "Why, man, they could hear you across Madison Square. You've a voice like an organ. Is it a 'go'?" he demanded.

"I don't think I quite understand," said the new-comer patiently.

"You don't, eh? Look there!"

FREDERIC STEWART ISHAM

A covered wagon had at that moment stopped before the door. It was drawn by a horse whose appearance, like that of the piano, spoke more eloquently of services in the past than of hopeful promises for the future. On the side of the vehicle appeared in large letters: "*What's the Matter with Mother?* Latest Melodic Triumph by America's Greatest Composer, Mr. Kerry Mackintosh." A little to the left of this announcement was painted a harp, probably a reminder of the one Saint Cecilia was supposed to have played. This sentimental symbol was obviously intended to lend dignity and respectability to the otherwise disreputable vehicle of concord and its steed without wings, waiting patiently to be off - or to lie down and pay the debt of nature!

"Shall we try it again, angel voice?" asked Mr. Mackintosh, playing the piano, or "biffing the ivories," as he called it.

"Drop it," returned the visitor, "that 'angel' dope."

"Oh, all right! Anything to oblige."

Before this vaguely apologetic reply, the new-comer once more relapsed into thoughtfulness. His eye passed dubiously over the vehicle of harmony; he began to take an interest in the front door as if again inclined to "back out." Perhaps a wish that the horse *might* lie down and die at this moment (no doubt he would be glad to!) percolated through the current of his thoughts. That would offer an easy solution to the proposal he imagined would soon be forthcoming - that *was* forthcoming - and accepted. Of course! What alternative remained? Needs must when an empty pocket drives. Had he not learned the lesson - beggars must not be choosers?

"And now," said Mr. Mackintosh with the air of a man who had cast from his shoulders a distinct problem, "that does away with the necessity of bailing the other chap out. What's your name?"

The visitor hesitated. "Horatio Heatherbloom."

The other looked at him keenly. "The right one," he said softly.

"You've got the only one you'll get," replied the caller, after an interval.

Mr. Mackintosh bestowed upon him a knowing wink. "Sounds like a *nom de plume*," he chuckled. "What was your line?"

"I don't understand."

"What did you serve time for? Shoplifting?"

"Oh, no," said the other calmly.

"Burglarizing?" With more respect in his tones.

"What do you think?" queried the caller in the same mild voice.

"Not ferocious-looking enough for that lay, I should have thought. However, you can't always tell by appearances. Now, I wonder -"

"What?" observed Mr. Heatherbloom, after an interval of silence.

"Yes! By Jove!" Mr. Mackintosh was speaking to himself. "It might work - it might add interest -" Mr. Heatherbloom waited patiently. "Would you have any objections," earnestly, "to my making a little addenda to the sign on the chariot of cadence? *What's the Matter with Mother*? 'The touching lyric, as interpreted by Horatio Heatherbloom, the reformed burglar'?"

"I *should* object," observed the caller.

"My boy - my boy! Don't be hasty. Take time to think. I'll go further; I'll paint a few iron bars in front of the harp. Suggestive of a prisoner in jail thinking of mother. Say 'yes'."

"No."

"Too bad!" murmured Mr. Mackintosh in disappointed but not altogether convinced tones. "You could use another alias, you know. If you're afraid the police might pipe your game and nab -"

"Drop it, or -"

"All right, Mr. Heatherbloom, or any other blooming name!" Recovering his jocular manner. "It's not for me to inquire the 'why,' or care a rap for the 'wherefore.' Ethics hasn't anything to do with the realm of art."

As he spoke he reached under the desk and took out the jug. "Have some?" extending the tumbler.

The thin lips of the other moved, his hand quickly extended but was drawn as suddenly back. "Thanks, but I'm on the water wagon, old chap."

"Well, I'm not. Do you know you said that just like a gentleman - to the manner born."

"A gentleman? A moment ago I was a reformed burglar."

"You might be both."

Mr. Heatherbloom looked into space; Mr. Mackintosh did not notice a subtle change of expression. That latter gentleman's rapt gaze was wholly absorbed by the half-tumblerful he held in mid air. But only for a moment; the next, he was smacking his lips. "We'll have a bite to eat and then go," he now said more cheerfully. "Ready for luncheon?"

"I could eat"

"Had anything to-day?"

"Maybe."

"And maybe, not!" Half jeeringly. "Why don't you say you've been training down, taking the go-without-breakfast cure? Say, it must be hell looking for a job when you've just 'got out'!"

"How do you know I just 'got out'?"

"You look it, and - there's a lot of reasons. Come on."

Half an hour or so later the covered wagon drove along Fourteenth street. Near the curb, not far from the corner of Broadway, it separated itself from the concourse of vehicles and stopped. Close by, nickel palaces of amusement exhibited their yawning entrances, and into these gilded maws floated, from the human current on the sidewalk, a stream of men, women and children. Encamped at the edge of this eddy, Mr. Mackintosh sounded on the nomadic piano, now ensconced within the coach of concord, the first triumphal strains of the maternal tribute in rag-time.

He and the conspiring instrument were concealed in the depths of the vehicle from the gaze of the multitude, but Mr. Heatherbloom at the back faced them on the little step which served as concert stage. There were no limelights or stereopticon pictures to add to the illusion, - only the disconcerting faces and the light of day. He never before knew how bright the day could be but he continued to stand there, in spite of the ludicrous and trying position. He sang, a certain daredevil light in his eye now, a suspicion of a covert smile on his face. It might be rather tragic - his position - but it was also a little funny.

His voice didn't sound any better out of doors than it did in; the "angel" quality of the white-robed choir days had departed with the soul of the boy. Perhaps Mr. Heatherbloom didn't really feel the pathos of the selection; at any rate, those tears Mr. Mackintosh had prophesied would be rolling down the cheeks of the listening multitude weren't forthcoming. One or two onlookers even laughed.

"Pigs! Swine!" murmured the composer, now passing through the crowd with copies of the song. He sold a few, not many; on the back step Mr. Heatherbloom watched with faint sardonic interest.

"Have I earned my luncheon yet?" he asked the composer when that aggrieved gentleman, jingling a few dimes, returned to the equipage of melody.

"Haven't counted up," was the gruff reply. "Give 'em another verse! They ain't accustomed to it yet. Once they git to know it, every boot-black in town will be whistling that song. Don't I know? Didn't I write it? Ain't they all had mothers?"

"Maybe they're all Topsies and 'just growed'," suggested Mr. Heatherbloom.

"Patience!" muttered the other. "The public may be a little coy at first, but once they git started they'll be fighting for copies. So encore, my boy; hammer it into them. We'll get them; you see!"

But the person addressed didn't see, at least with Mr. Mackintosh's clairvoyant vision. Mr. Heatherbloom's gaze wandering quizzically from the little pool of mask-like faces had rested on a great shining motor-car approaching - slowly, on account of the press of traffic. In this wide luxurious vehicle reposed a young girl, slender, exquisite; at her side sat a big, dark, distinguished-appearing man, with a closely cropped black beard; a foreigner - most likely Russian.

The girl was as beautiful as the dainty orchids with which the superb car was adorned, and which she, also, wore in her gown - yellow orchids, tenderly fashioned but very insistent and bright. Upon this patrician vision Mr. Heatherbloom had inadvertently looked, and the pathetic plaint regarding "Mother" died on the wings of nothingness. With unfilial respect he literally abandoned her and cast her to the winds. His eyes gleamed as they rested on the girl; he seemed to lose himself in reverie.

Did she, the vision in orchids, notice him? Perhaps! The chauffeur at that moment increased the speed of the big car; but as it dashed past, the crimson mouth of the beautiful girl tightened and hardened into a straight line and those wonderful starlike eyes shone suddenly with a light as hard as steel. Disdainful, contemptuous; albeit, perhaps, passionate! Then she, orchids, shining car and all were whirled on.

Rattle! bang! went the iron-rimmed wheels of other rougher vehicles. Bing! bang! sounded the piano like a soul in torment.

Horatio Heatherbloom stood motionless; then his figure swayed slightly. He lifted the music, as if to shield his features from the others - his many auditors; but they didn't mind that brief interruption; it afforded a moment for that rough and ready dialogue which a gathering of this kind finds to its liking.

"Give him a trokee! Anybody got a cough drop?"

"It's soothing syrup he wants."

"No; it's us wants that."

"What the devil -" Mr. Mackintosh looked out of the wagon.

Mr. Heatherbloom suddenly laughed, a forced reckless laugh. "Guess it was the dampness. I'm like some artists - have to be careful where I sing."

"Have a tablet, feller, do!" said a man in the audience.

Horatio looked him in the eye. "Maybe it's you

want something."

The facetious one began to back away; he had seen that look before, the steely glint that goes before battle.

"The chord now, if you please!" said Mr. Heatherbloom to the composer in a still quiet voice.

Mr. Mackintosh hit viciously; Mr. Heatherbloom sang again; he did more than that. He outdid himself; he employed bombast, - some thought it pathos. He threw a tremolo into his voice; it passed for emotion. He "caught 'em", in Mr. Mackintosh's parlance, and "caught 'em hard". Some more people bought copies. The alert Mr. Mackintosh managed to gather in about a dollar, and saw, in consequence, great fortune "coming his way" at last; the clouds had a golden lining.

"Say, you're the pard I've been a-looking for!" he jubilantly told Mr. Heatherbloom as they prepared to move on. "We'll make a beautiful team. Isn't it a peach?"

"What?"

"That song. It made them look like a rainy day. Git up!" And Mr. Mackintosh prodded the bony ribs of their steed.

Mr. Heatherbloom absent-mindedly gazed in the direction the big shining motor had vanished.

CHAPTER II

VARYING FORTUNES

Mr. Heatherbloom's new-found employment proved but ephemeral. The next day the sheriff took possession of the music emporium and all it contained, including the nomadic piano and the now empty jug. The contents of the last the composer-publisher took care to put beyond reach of his many creditors whom he, in consequence, faced with a seemingly care-free, if artificial, jocularity. Mr. Heatherbloom walked soberly forth from the shop of concord.

He had but turned the corner of the street when into the now dissonant "hole in the wall", amid the scene of wreck and disaster, stepped a tall dark man, with a closely cropped beard, who spoke English with an accent and who regarded the erstwhile proprietor and the minions of the law with ill-concealed arrogance and disfavor.

"You have," he began in halting tones, "a young man here who sings on the street like the minstrels of old, the - what you call them? - troubadours."

"We *had*," corrected Mr. Mackintosh. "He has just 'jumped the coup,' or rather been 'shooed out'."

The new-comer fastened his gaze upon the other; he had superb, almost mesmeric eyes. "Will you kindly speak the language as I understand it?" he said. And the other did, for there was that in the caller's manner which compelled immediate compliance. Immovably he listened to the composer-publisher's explanation.

"*Eh bien!*" he said, his handsome, rather barbaric head high when Mr. Mackintosh had concluded. "He is gone; it is well; I have fulfilled my mission." And walking out, the imposing stranger hailed a taxi and disappeared from the neighborhood.

Meanwhile Mr. Horatio Heatherbloom had walked slowly on; he was now some distance from the one-time "emporium." Where should he go? His fortunes had not been enhanced materially by his brief excursion into the realms of melody; he had thirty cents in cash and a "dollar-and-a-half appetite." An untidy place where they displayed a bargain assortment of creature comforts attracted his gaze. He thought of meals in the past - of caviar, a la Russe, three dollars and a half a portion; peaches Melba, three francs each at the Cafe de Paris; truffled capon from Normandy; duck after the manner of the incomparable Frederic. About half a dozen peaches Melba would have appealed to him now; he looked, instead, with the eyes of longing at a codfish ball. Oh, glorious appetite, mocking recollections of hours of satiety!

Should he yield to temptation? He stopped; then prudence prevailed. The day was yet too young to give way recklessly to casual gastronomic allurements, so he stepped on again quickly, averting his head from shop windows. Lest his caution and conservatism might give way, he started to turn into a side street - but didn't.

Instead, he laughed slightly to himself. What! flee from an outpost of time-worn celery? beat an inglorious retreat before a phalanx of machine-made pies? He would look them (figuratively) in the eye. Having, as it were, fairly stared out of countenance the bland pies and beamed with stern contempt upon the "droopy," Preraphaelite celery, he went, better satisfied, on his way. It is these little victories that count; at that moment Mr. Heatherbloom marched on like a knight of old for steadfastness of purpose. His lips veiled a covert smile, as if behind the hard mask of life he saw something a little odd and whimsical, appealing to some secret sense of humor that even hunger could not wholly annihilate. The lock of hair seemed to droop rather pathetically at that moment; his sensitive features were slightly pinched; his face was pale. It would probably be paler before the day was over; *n'importe!* The future had to be met - for better, or worse. Multitudes passed this way and that; an elevated went crashing by; devastating influences seemed to surround him. His slender form stiffened.

When next he stopped it was to linger, not in front of an eating establishment, but before a bulletin-board upon which was pasted a page of newspaper "want ads" for "trained" men, in all walks of life. "Trained" men? Hateful word! How often had he encountered it! Ah, here was one advertisement without the "trained"; he devoured it eagerly. The item, like an oasis in the desert of his general incapacity and uselessness, exercised an odd fascination for him in spite of the absolute impossibility of his professing to possess a fractional part of those moral attributes demanded by the fair advertiser. She - a Miss Van Rolsen - was seeking a paragon, not a person. Nevertheless, he resolved to assail the apparently unassailable, and repaired to a certain ultrafashionable neighborhood of the town.

Before a brownstone front that bore the number he sought, he paused a moment, drew a deep breath and started to walk up the front steps. But with a short laugh he came suddenly to a halt half-way up; looked over the stone balustrade down at the other entrance below - the tradesmen's - the butchers', the bakers', the candlestick makers' - and, yes, the servants' - their way in! - his?

He went down the steps and walked on and away as a matter of course, but once more stopped. He had done a good deal of going this way and that, and then stopping, during the last few months. Things had to be worked out, and sometimes his brain didn't seem to move very quickly.

To be worked out! He now surveyed the butchers' and the bakers' (and yes, the servants') entrance with casual or philosophic interest from the vantage point of the other side of the street. It wasn't different from any other of the entrances of the kind but it held his gaze. Then he walked across the street again and went in - or down. It didn't really seem now such a bad kind of entrance when you came to investigate it, in a high impersonal way; not half so bad as the subway, and people didn't mind that.

Still Mr. Heatherbloom experienced a peculiar thrill when he put up his thumb, pressed a button, and wondered what next would happen. Who answered doors down here, - the maid - the cook - the laundress?

FREDERIC STEWART ISHAM

He felt himself to be very indistinct and vague standing there in the shadow, and tried to assume a nonchalant bearing. He wondered just what bearing *was* proper under the circumstances; he cherished indistinct recollections of having heard or read that the butcher's boy is usually favored with a broadly defying and independent visage; that he comes in whistling and goes forth swaggering. A cat-meat man he had once looked upon from the upper lodge of front steps somewhere in the dim long ago, had possessed a melancholy manner and countenance.

How should he comport himself; what should he say - when the inevitable happened; when the time came to say something? How lead the conversation by natural and easy stages to the purport of his visit? He rehearsed a few sentences, then straightway forgot them. Why did they keep him waiting so long? Did they always keep people as long as that - down here? He put his thumb again -

"Well, what do you want?" The door had opened and a buxom female, arms akimbo, regarded him. Mr. Heatherbloom repaid her gaze with interest; it *was* the cook, then, who acted as door tender of these regions subterranean. He feared by her expression that he had interrupted her in the preparation of some esculent delicacy, and with the fear was born a parenthetical inquiry; he wondered what that delicacy might be? But forbearing to inquire he stated his business.

"You'll be the thirteenth that's been 'turned down' to-day for that job!" observed cook blandly. With which cheering assurance she consigned him to some one else - a maid with a tipped-up nose - and presently he found himself being "shown up"; that was the expression used.

The room into which he was ushered was a parlor. Absently he seated himself. The maid tittered. He looked at her - or rather the tipped-up nose, an attractive bit of anatomy. Saucy, provocative! Mr. Heatherbloom's head tilted a little; he surveyed the detail with the look of a connoisseur. She colored, went; but remained in the hall to peer. There were many articles of virtu lying around - on tables or in cabinets - and the caller's appearance was against him. He would bear watching; he had the impudence - Just fancy his sitting there in a chair! He was leaning back now as if he enjoyed that atmosphere of luxury; surveying, too, the paintings and the bronzes with interest. But for no good reason, thought the maid; then gave a start of surprise. The hand of the suspicious-looking caller had lifted involuntarily to his breast pocket; a mechanical movement such as a young gentleman might make who was reaching for a cigarette case. Did he intend - actually intend to - but the caller's hand fell; he sat forward suddenly on the edge of his chair and seemed for the first time aware that his attitude partook of the anomalous; for gathering up his shabby hat from the gorgeous rug, he abruptly rose.

Just in time to confront, or be confronted by, an austere lady in stiff satin or brocade and with bristling iron-gray hair! He noticed, however, that unlike the maid, she had a very prominent nose - that *now* sniffed!

"Good heavens! What a frightful odor of gasolene. Jane, where are my salts?"

Jane rushed in; at the same time four or five dogs that

had followed in the lady's wake began to bark as if they, too, were echoing the plaint: "What a frightful odor! Salts, Jane, salts!" And as they barked in many keys, but always fortissimo, they ran frantically this way and that as though chased by somebody, or something (perhaps the odor of gasolene), or chasing one another in a mad outburst of canine exuberance.

"Sardanapolis! Beauty! Curly! Naughty!" the lady called out.

But in vain. Sardanapolis continued to cut capers; Beauty's conduct was not beautiful; while as for Naughty (all yellow bows and black curls) he seemed endeavoring to live up to the fullest realization of his name.

"Dear me! What *shall* I do?"

"Just let 'em alone, ma'am," ventured Jane, "and they'll soon tire themselves out."

Fortunately, by this time, the be-ribboned pets showed signs of reaching that state of ennui.

"Dear me!" said now the lady anxiously. "How wet the poor dears' tongues are!"

"Nature of the b - poor dears, ma'am!" commented Jane.

The lady looked at her. "*You* don't like dogs," she said. "You can go." And then to Mr. Heatherbloom: "What brought you here? Don't answer at once. Stand farther back."

Mr. Heatherbloom, who seemed to have been rather enjoying this little impromptu entertainment, straightened with a start; he retired a few paces, observing in a mild explanatory tone something about spots on his garments and the necessity for having them removed at a certain little Greek shop, before doing himself the honor of calling and -

"You're another answer to the advertisement then, I suppose?" the lady's voice unceremoniously interrupted.

He confessed himself Another Answer, and in that capacity proceeded now to reply as best he might to a merciless and rapid fire of questions. She would have made an excellent cross-examiner for the prosecution; Mr. Heatherbloom did not seem to enjoy the grilling. A number of queries he answered frankly; others he evaded. He seemed - ominous circumstance! - especially secretive regarding certain details of his past. He did not care to say where he was born, or who his parents were. What had he done? What occupations had he followed?

Well - he seemed to hesitate a good deal - he had once tried washing dishes; but - dreamily - they had discharged him; the man said something about there being a debit balance on account of damaged crockery. He had essayed the role of waiter but had lasted only through the first courses; down to the entrees, he thought; certainly not much past the pottage. He believed he bumped into another waiter; a few guests within range had seemed put out; afterward, he himself was put out. And then - well, he had somehow drifted, more or less.

"Drifted!" said the lady ominously.

"Oh, yes! Tried his hand at this and that," he added rather blithely. He once worked for a moving-picture firm; fell from a six-story window for them. That is, he started to fall; something - a net or a platform - was supposed to catch him at the fifth, and then a dummy completed the descent and got smashed on the sidewalk. He was a little doubtful about their intercepting him at the fifth and that he, instead of the dummy - But he didn't seem to mind taking the risk - reflectively. They said he was a great success falling through the air, and they had him, in consequence, fall from all kinds of places, - through drawbridges into the water, for example. That's where he contracted a bad cold, and when he had recovered, another man had been found for the heavier-than-air role -

"What are you talking about?" The lady's back was stiffer than a poker.

"If ever you go to a moving-picture palace of amusement, Madam, and see a streak in the air, you might reasonably conclude you are" - he bowed - "beholding me. I went once; it seemed funny. I hardly recognized myself in the part. I certainly seemed to be 'going some'," he murmured seriously. "Is there anything else, Madam, you would care to question me about?"

"I think," she said significantly, "what I have learned is quite sufficient. If the occupations you have told me about are so disreputable - what were those you have kept so carefully concealed? For example, where were you and what were you doing four - five - six - years ago? You have already refused to answer. You relate only a few inconsequential and outre trifles. To cover up - What? What?" she repeated.

Then she transfixed him with her eye; the dogs transfixed him with their eyes. Accusingly? Not all of them. Naughty's glance expressed approval; his tail underwent a friendly agitation.

"Naughty!" said the lady sharply. Naughty gamboled around Horatio.

"How odd!" murmured the mistress, more to herself than the other. "How very extraordinary!"

"What, Madam?" he ventured.

"That Naughty, who so seldom takes to strangers, should -" she found herself saying.

"Perhaps it's the scent of the gasolene," he suggested.

"It's *in spite of* the gasolene," she retorted sharply.

And for some moments ruminated. It was not until afterward Mr. Heatherbloom learned that her confidence in Naughty's instinct amounted to a hobby. Only once had she thought him at fault in his likes or dislikes of people; when he had showed a predilection for the assistant rector's shapely calves. But after that gentleman's elopement with a lady of the choir and his desertion of wife and children, Naughty's erstwhile disrespect for the cloth, which Miss Van Rolsen had grieved over, became illumined with force and significance. Thereafter she had never doubted him; he had barked at all twelve of Mr. Heatherbloom's predecessors - the dozen other answers to the advertisement; but here he was sedulous for fondlings from Horatio.

FREDERIC STEWART ISHAM

Extraordinary truly! The lady hesitated.

"I suppose we shall all be murdered in our beds," she said half to herself, "but," with sudden decision, "I've concluded to engage you."

"And my duties?" ventured Mr. Heatherbloom. "The advertisement did not say."

"You are to exercise the darlings every day in the park."

"Ah!" Horatio's exclamation was noncommittal. What he might have added was interrupted by a light footstep in the hall and the voice of some one who stopped in passing before the door.

"I am going now, Aunt," said a voice.

Mr. Heatherbloom started; his hand tightened on the back of a chair; from where he stood he could see but the rim of a wonderful hat. He gazed at a few waving roses, fitting notes of color as it were, for the lovely face behind, concealed from him by the curtain.

The elderly lady answered; Mr. Heatherbloom heard a Prince Someone's name mentioned; then the roses were whisked back; the voice - musical as silver bells - receded, and the front door closed. Mr. Heatherbloom gazed around him - at the furnishings in the room - she who stood before him. He seemed bewildered.

"And now as to your wages," said a voice - not silver bells! - sharply.

"I hardly think I should prove suitable -" he began in

somewhat panic-stricken tones, when -

"Nonsense!" The word, or the energy imparted to it, appeared to crush for the moment further opposition on his part; his faculties became concentrated on a sound without, of a big car gathering headway in front of the door. Mr. Heatherbloom listened; perhaps he would have liked to retreat then and there from that house; but it was too late! Fate had precipitated him here. A mad tragic jest! He did not catch the amount of his proposed stipend that was mentioned; he even forgot for the moment he was hungry. He could no longer hear the car. It had gone; but, it would return. Return! And then -? His head whirled at the thought.

CHAPTER III

AN ENCOUNTER

Mr. Heatherbloom, a few days later, sat one morning in Central Park. His canine charges were tied to the bench and while they chafed at restraint and tried vainly to get away and chase squirrels, he scrutinized one of the pages of a newspaper some person had left there. What the young man read seemed to give him no great pleasure. He put down the paper; then picked it up again and regarded a snap-shot illustration occupying a conspicuous position on the society page.

"Prince Boris Strogareff, riding in the park," the picture was labeled. The newspaper photographer had caught for his sensational sheet an excellent likeness of a foreign visitor in whom New York was at the time greatly interested. A picturesque personality - the prince - half distinguished gentleman, half bold brigand in appearance, was depicted on a superb bay, and looked every inch a horseman. Mr. Heatherbloom continued to stare at the likeness; the features, dark, rather wild-looking, as if a trace of his ancient Tartar ancestry had survived the cultivating touch of time. Then the young man on the bench once more turned his attention to the text accompanying the cut.

"Reported engagement of Miss Elizabeth Dalrymple to

Prince Boris Strogareff ... the prince has vast estates in Russia and Russia-Asia ... his forbears were prominent in the days when Crakow was building and the Cossacks and the Poles were engaged in constant strife on the steppe ... Miss Dalrymple, with whom this stalwart romantic personage is said to be deeply enamored, is niece and heiress of the eccentric Miss Van Rolsen, the third richest woman in New York, and, probably, in the world ... Miss Dalrymple is the only surviving daughter of Charles Dalrymple of San Francisco, who made his fortune with Martin Ferguson of the same place, at the time -"

The paper fell from Mr. Heatherbloom's hand; for several moments he sat motionless; then he got up, unloosened his charges and moved on. They naturally became once more wild with joy, but he heeded not their exuberances; even Naughty's demonstrations brought no answering touch of his hand, that now lifted to his breast and took something from his pocket - an article wrapped in a pink tissue-paper. Mr. Heatherbloom unfolded the warm-tinted covering with light sedulous fingers and looked steadily and earnestly at a miniature. But only for a brief interval; by this time Curly et al. had become an incomprehensible tangle of dog and leading strings about Mr. Heather-bloom's legs. So much so, indeed, that in the effort to extricate himself he dropped the tiny picture; with a sudden passionate exclamation he stooped for it. The anger that transformed his usually mild visage seemed about to vent itself on his charges but almost at once subsided.

Carefully brushing the picture on his coat, he replaced it in his pocket and quietly started to disentangle his charges from himself. This was at length accomplished; he knew, however, that the unraveling would have to be done all over again ere long; it constituted an important part of his duties. The promenade was punctuated by about so many "mix-ups"; Mr. Heatherbloom accepted them philosophically, or absent-mindedly. At any rate, while untying knots or disengaging things, he usually exhibited much patience.

It might have been noticed some time later that Mr. Heatherbloom, retracing his footsteps to Miss Van Rolsen's, betrayed a rather vacillating and uncertain manner, as if he were somewhat reluctant to go into, or to approach too near the old-fashioned stiff and stately house. For fear of meeting some one, or a dread of some sudden encounter? With Miss Van Rolsen's niece? So far he had not seen her since that first day. Perhaps he congratulated himself on his good fortune in this respect. If so, he reckoned without his host.

It is possible for two people to frequent the same house for quite a while without meeting when one of them lives on the avenue side and flits back and forth via the front steps, while the other comes and goes only by the subterranean route; but, sooner or later, though belonging to widely different worlds, these two are bound to come face to face, even in spite of the determination of one of the persons to avert such a contingency!

Mr. Heatherbloom always peered carefully about before venturing from the house with his pampered charges; he was no less watchfully alert when he returned. He could not, however, having only five senses, tell when the front door might be suddenly opened at an inopportune moment. It was opened, this very morning, on the third day of his probation at such a moment. And he had been planning, after reading the newspaper article in the park, to tender his resignation that very afternoon!

It availed him nothing now to regret indecision, his being partly coerced by the masterful mistress of the house into remaining as long as he had remained; or to lament that other sentiment, conspiring to this end - the desire or determination, not to flee from what he most feared. Empty bravado! If he could but flee now! But there was no fleeing, turning, retreating, or evading. The issue had to be met.

Miss Dalrymple, gowned in a filmy material which lent an evanescent charm to her slender figure, came down the front steps as he was about to enter the area way below. The girl looked at him and her eyes suddenly widened; she stopped. Mr. Heatherbloom, quite pale, bowed and would have gone on, when something in her look, or the first word that fell from her lips, held him.

"You!" she said, as if she did not at all comprehend.

He repaid her regard with less steady look; he had to say something and he didn't wish to. Why couldn't people just meet and pass on, the way dumb creatures do? The gift of speech has its disadvantages - on occasions; it forces one to insufficient answer or superfluous explanation. "Yes," he said, "your - Miss Van Rolsen engaged me. I didn't really want to stay, but it came about. Some things do, you know. You see," he added, "I didn't know she was your aunt when I answered the advertisement."

She bent her gaze down upon him as if she hardly heard; beneath the bright adornment of tints, the lovely face - it was a very proud face - had become icy cold; the violet eyes were hard as shining crystal. To Mr. Heatherbloom that slender figure, tensely poised, seemed at once overwhelmingly near and inexpressibly remote. He started to lean on an iron picket but changed his mind and stood rather too stiffly, without support. Before his eyes the flowers in her hat waved and waved; he tried to keep his eyes on them.

"I had been intending," he observed in tones he endeavored to make light, "to tell Miss Van Rolsen she must find some one else to take my place. It would not be very difficult. It is not a position that requires a trained man."

"Difficult?" She seemed to have difficulty in speaking the word; her cold eyes suddenly lighted with unutterable scorn. If any one in this world ever experienced thorough disdain for any one else, her expression implied it was she that experienced it for him. "Valet for dogs!"

Mr. Heatherbloom flushed. "They are very nice dogs," he murmured. "Indeed, they are exceptional."

She gave an abrupt, frozen little laugh; then bent down her face slightly. "And do you wash and curl and perfume them?" she asked, her small white teeth setting tightly after she spoke.

"Well, I don't perfume them," answered Mr. Heatherbloom. "Miss Van Rolsen attends to that herself. She knows the particular essences better than I." A slightly strained smile struggled about his lips. "You see

Beauty has one kind, and Naughty another. At least, I think so. While Sardanapolis isn't given any at all."

Can violet eyes shine fiercely? Hers certainly seemed to. "How," she said, examining him as one would study something very remote and impersonal, "did my aunt happen to employ - you? I know she is very particular - about recommendations. What ones did you have? Were they forged ones," suddenly, "or stolen ones?" The red lips like rosebuds had become straightly drawn now.

"No," answered Mr. Heatherbloom. "I didn't have any. I just came, and -"

"Saw and conquered!" said the girl. But there was no levity in her tone. She continued to gaze at him and yet through him; at something beyond - afar - "I don't understand why she should have taken you -"

"Shall I explain?"

"And I don't care why she did!" Not noticing his interruption. "The principal thing is, why did you want this position? What ulterior motive lay behind?" She was speaking now almost automatically, as if he were not present. "For, of course, there was some other motive."

"The truth is," observed Mr. Heatherbloom lightly, but passing an uncertain hand over his brow, "I had reached that point - I should qualify by saying I have long been at the point where one is willing to take any 'honest work of any kind'. I suppose you have heard the phrase before; it's a common one. But believe me, it was quite by accident I came here; quite!"

"'Believe you'," said the girl, as one would address an inferior for the purpose of putting him into the category where he belongs. "'Honest work'! When have you been particular as to that; whether or not" - with mocking irony in the pitiless violet eyes - "it was 'honest'?"

Mr. Heatherbloom started; his gaze met hers unwaveringly. "You don't think, then, that I -"

"Think?" said the girl. "I know."

"Would you mind - explaining?" he asked quietly. He didn't need any support now, but stood with head well back, a steady gleam in his look. "What you - know?"

"I know - you are a thief!" She spoke the Words fiercely.

His face twitched. "How do you know?"

"By the kind of evidence I can believe."

"And that?" he said in the same quiet voice.

"The evidence of my own eyes!"

He was still, as if thinking. He looked down; then away.

"Why don't you protest?" she demanded.

"Protest," he repeated.

"Or ask me to explain further -"

"Well, explain further," he said patiently.

"Put your mind back three weeks ago - at about eleven o'clock in the morning. Where were you? what were you doing? what was happening?"

Mr. Heatherbloom looked very thoughtful.

"At the corner of" - she mentioned the streets - "not far from Riverside Drive. We passed at that time in the car. Need I say more?"

His head was downbent. "I think I understand." His hand stroked tentatively his chin.

The silence grew; Beauty barked, but neither seemed to notice.

"Of course you can't deny?" she observed.

"Of course not," he said, without moving.

"You won't defend yourself; plead palliating causes?" ironically.

He picked at the ground with the toe of a shoe. "If I told you, on my honor, I am not - what you have called me just now, would you believe me?" he asked gravely.

"On your honor," said the girl with a cruel smile. "Yours? No!"

"Then," he spoke as if to himself, " I don't suppose there's any use in denying. Your mind is made up."

"My mind!" she answered. "Can I not see; hear? Can *you* not hear - those voices? Do they not follow you?"

He seemed striving for an answer but could not find it. Once he looked into the violet eyes questioningly, deeply, as if seeking there to read what he should say, but they flashed only the hard rays of diamonds at him, and he turned his head slowly away.

"I see," she remarked, "you remember; but you do not care."

"I - you reconcile the idea of my being *that* very easily with -"

"It fits perfectly," said the girl, "with the rest of the picture; what one has already pieced together; it is just another odd-shaped black bit that goes in snugly. You appreciate the comparison?"

"I think I do," answered Mr. Heatherbloom. "You are alluding to picture puzzles. Is there anything more?" He started as if to go.

"One moment - of course, you can't stay here," said the girl.

"I had intended to go at once, as I told you," observed Mr. Heatherbloom.

"You had? You mean you will?"

"No; I won't go now. That is," he added, "of my own volition."

"You do well to qualify. Would you not prefer to go of

your own volition than to have me inform my aunt who you are - what you are?"

He shook his head. "I won't resign now," he said.

"And so show yourself a fool as well as -" She did not speak the word, but it trembled on the sweet passionate lips.

He did not answer.

"Suppose," she went on, "I offer you the chance and do not speak, if you will go - immediately?"

"I can't," he answered.

Her brows bent; her little hand seemed to clench. But he stood without looking at her, appearing absorbed in a tiny bit of cloud in the sky.

"Very well!" she said, a dangerous glint in her eyes.

He looked quite insignificant at the moment; she was far above him; his clothes were threadbare, the way thieves' clothes, or pickpockets', usually are.

"If you expect any mercy from me -" she began.

But she did not finish; a figure, approaching, caught her eye - the handsome stalwart figure of a man; whose features lighted at sight of her.

"Ah, Miss Dalrymple!"

Her face changed. "An unexpected pleasure, Prince," she said with almost an excess of gaiety.

FREDERIC STEWART ISHAM

He answered in kind; she came down the steps quickly, offering him her hand. And as he gallantly raised the small perfumed fingers to his lips, Mr. Heatherbloom seemed to fade away into the dark subterranean entrance.

CHAPTER IV

FATE AT THE DOOR

Although Mr. Heatherbloom waited expectantly that day for his dismissal, it did not come. This surprised him somewhat; then he reflected that Miss Elizabeth Dalrymple was probably so absorbed in the prince - remembering her rather effusive greeting of that fortunate individual - she had forgotten such a small matter as having the dog valet ejected from the premises. She would remember on the morrow, of course.

But she didn't! The hours passed, and he was suffered to go about the even, or uneven, tenor of his way. This he did mechanically; he scrubbed and combed Beauty beautifully. With a dire sense of fate knocking at the door, he passed her on to Miss Van Rolsen, to be freshly be-ribboned by that lady's own particular hand. The thin bony finger he thought would be pointed accusingly at him, busied itself solely with the knots and bows of a new ribbon; after which the grim lady dismissed him - from her presence, not the house - curtly.

Several days went by; still no one accused him; he was still suffered to remain. Why? He could not understand. At the end of a long - seemingly interminable week - he put himself deliberately in the way of finding out. Coming to, or going from the house, he lingered around the area entrance, purposely to encounter her whom he had heretofore, above all others, wished to avoid. A feverish desire possessed him to meet the worst, and then go about his way, no matter where it might lead him. He was past solicitude in that regard. He did at length manage to meet her - not as before in the full daylight but toward dusk, as she returned, this time on foot, to the house.

"Miss Dalrymple, may I speak to you?" he said to the indistinctly seen, slender figure that started lightly up the front steps.

She did not even stop, although she must have heard him; a moment he saw her like a shadow; then the front door opened. He heard a crisp metallic click; the door closed. Slowly with head a little downbent he walked out, up the way she had come; then around the corner a short distance to the stables over which he had his room.

It was a nice room, he had at first thought, probably because he liked horses. They - four or five thorough-breds - whinnied as he opened the door. He had started up the dark narrow stairs to his chamber, but stopped at that sound and groped about from stall to stall passing around the expected lumps of sugar. After which all seemed well as far as he and they were concerned.

Only that other problem! - he could not shake it from him. To resign now? - under fire? How he wished he might! But to remain? - his situation was intolerable. He went up to his room feeling like a ghost; his mind was full of dark presences, as if he had lived a thousand times before and had been surrounded only by hostile influences that now came back in the still watches of the night to haunt him.

He dreaded going to the house the next day, but he went. Perhaps, he reflected, she was only allowing him to retain his present position under a kind of espionage; to trap him and put him beyond the pale of respectable society. He remembered the cruel lips, the passionate dislike - contempt - even hatred - in her eyes. Yes; that might be it - the reason for her temporary silence; the house was full of valuable things; sooner or later -

"Are you quite satisfied, Madam, with my services?" said Mr. Heatherbloom that afternoon to Miss Van Rolsen.

"You seem to do well enough," she answered shortly.

He brightened. "Perhaps some one else would do better."

"Perhaps," she returned dryly. "But I'm not going to try."

"But," he said desperately, "I - I don't think they - the dogs, like me quite so much as they did. Naughty, in particular," he added quickly. "I - I thought yesterday he would have liked to - growl and nip at me."

"Did he," she asked, studying him with disconcerting keenness, "actually do that?"

"No. But -"

"Do I understand you wish to give me notice?" she

FREDERIC STEWART ISHAM

interrupted sharply.

"Not at all." In an alarmed tone. "I couldn't - I mean I wouldn't do that. Only I thought you might have felt dissatisfied - people usually do with me," he added impressively. "So if you would like to give me -"

She made a gesture. "That will do. I am very busy this morning. The begging list, though smaller than usual - only three hundred and seventy-six letters - has to be attended to."

Thus the matter of Mr. Heatherbloom's staying or going continued, much to that person's discomfiture, *in statu quo*. It is true he found, later, a compromising course; a way out of the difficulty - as he thought, little knowing the extraordinary new web he was weaving! - but before that time came, several things happened. In the first place he discovered that Miss Dalrymple was not entirely pleased at the publication of the story of her engagement to the prince; her position - her family's and that of Miss Van Rolsen, was such that newspaper advertising or notoriety could not but be distasteful.

"I hope people won't think I keep a social secretary," Mr. Heatherbloom heard her say.

Yes, heard her. He was in the dogs' "boudoir"; the conservatory adjoined. He could not help being where he was; he belonged there at the time. Nor could he help hearing; he didn't try to listen; he certainly didn't wish to, though she had a very sweet voice - that soothed one to a species of lotus dream - forgetfulness of soap-suds, or the odor of canine disinfectant permeating the white foam -

"Why should they think you have a social secretary?" the voice of a man - the prince - inquired.

He had deep fine tones; truly Russian tones, with a subtle vibration in them.

"Because when such things are published about people their secretaries usually put them in," returned the girl.

He was silent a moment; Mr. Heatherbloom thought he heard the breaking of the stem of a flower.

"You were very much irritated - angry?" observed the prince at length, quietly.

"Weren't you?" she asked.

"I? No. It is a bourgeois confession, perhaps."

Mr. Heatherbloom sat up straighter; the water dripped from his fingers.

"I was pleased," went on the sonorous low voice. "I wished - it were so!"

There was a sudden movement in the conservatory; a rustling of leaves, or of a gown; then - Mr. Heatherbloom relaxed in surprise - a peal of merry laughter filled the air.

"How apropos! How well you said that!"

"Miss Dalrymple!" There was a slightly rising inflection in the man's tones. "You doubt my sincerity?"

"The sincerity of a Russian prince? No, indeed!" she returned gaily.

"I am in earnest," he said simply.

"Don't be!" Mr. Heatherbloom could, in fancy, see the flash of a white hand amid red flowers; eyes dancing like violets in the wind. He could perceive, also, as plainly as if he were in that other room, the deep ardent eyes of the prince downbent upon the blither ones, the commanding figure of the man near that other slender, almost illusive presence. A flower to be grasped only by a bold wooer, like the prince!

"Don't be," she repeated. "You are so much more charming when you are not. I think I heard that line in a play once. One of the Robertson kind; it was given by a stock company in San Francisco. That's where I came from, you know. Have you ever been there?"

"No," said the prince slowly.

Dark eyes trying to beat down the merriment in the blue ones! Mr. Heatherbloom could, in imagination, "fill in" all the stage details. If it only were "stage" dialogue; "stage" talk; not "playing with love", in earnest!

"Playing with love!" He had read a book of that name once; somewhere. In Italy? - yes. It sounded like an Italian title. Something very disagreeable happened to the heroine. A woman, or a girl, can not lightly "play with love" with a Sicilian. But, of course, the prince wasn't a Sicilian.

"No," he was saying now with admirable poise, in

answer to her question, "I haven't visited your wonderful Golden Gate, but I hope to go there some day - with you!" he added. His words were simple; the accent alone made them sound formidable; it seemed to convey an impregnable purpose, one not to be shaken or disturbed.

Mr. Heatherbloom felt vaguely disturbed; his heart pounded oddly. He half started to get up, then sank back. He waited for another peal of laughter; it didn't come. Why?

"Of course I should have no objection to your being one of a train party," said Miss Dalrymple at length.

"That isn't just what I mean," returned the prince in his courtliest tones. But it wasn't hard to picture him now with a glitter in his gaze, - immovable, sure of himself.

There was a rather long pause; broken once more by Miss Dalrymple: "Shall we not return to the music room?"

That interval? What had it meant? Mute acquiescence on her part, a down-turning of the imperious lashes before the steadfastness of the other's look? - tacit assent? The casting off of barriers, the opening of the gates of the divine inner citadel? Mr. Heatherbloom was on his feet now. He took a step toward the door, but paused. Of course! Something clammy had fallen from his hand; lay damp and dripping on the rag. He stared at it - a bar of soap.

What had he been about to do - he! - to step in there - into the conservatory, with his bar of soap? - grotesque anomaly! His face wore a strange expression; he was laughing inwardly. Oh, how he was laughing at himself! Fortunately he had a saving sense of humor.

What had next been said in the conservatory? What was now being said there? He heard words but they had no meaning for him. "I will send you the second volume of *The Fire and Sword* trilogy," went on the prince. "One of my ancestors figures in it. The hero - who is not exactly a hero, perhaps, in the heroine's mind, for a time - does what he must do; he has what he must have. He claims what nature made for him; he knows no other law than that of his imperishable inner self. I, too, must rise to those heights my eyes are set on. It must be; it is written. We are fatalists, we Russians near the Tartar line! And you and I" - fervently - "were predestined for each other."

Mr. Heatherbloom had but dimly heard the prince's words and failed to grasp them; he didn't want to; his head was humming. Her light answer sounded as if she might be very happy. Yes; naturally. She was made to be happy, to dance about like sunshine. He liked to think of the picture. The prince, too, was necessary to complete it; necessary, reaffirmed Mr. Heatherbloom to himself, pulling with damp fingers at the inconsequential lock of hair over his brow. Of course, if the prince could be eliminated from that mental picture of her felicity? - but he was a part of the composition; big, barbaric, romantic looking! In fact, it wouldn't have been an adequate composition at all without him; no, indeed!

And something rose in Mr. Heatherbloom's throat; one of his eyes - or was it both of them? - seemed a little misty. That confounded soap! It was strong; a bit of it in the corner of the eyes made one blink.

The two in the conservatory said something more; but the young man in the "boudoir" didn't catch it at all well. By some intense mental process, or the sound of the scrubber on the edge of the tub, he found he could shut a definite cognizance of words almost entirely from his sense of hearing. The prince's voice seemed slightly louder; that, in a general way, was patent; no doubt the occasion warranted more fervor on his part. Mr. Heatherbloom tried to imagine what she would look like in - so to say, a very complaisant mood; not with flaming glance full of aversion and scorn!

Violet eyes replete only with love lights! Mr. Heatherbloom bent lower over the tub; his four-footed charge Beauty, contentedly immersed to the neck in nice comfortably warm water, licked him. He did not feel the touch; the fragrance of orchids seemed to come to him above that other more healthful, less agreeable odor of special cleansing preparation.

Her accents were heard once more. Those final words sounded like a soft command. Naturally! She could command the prince - now! Mr. Heatherbloom heard a door close - a replica of the harsh click he had listened to when she had shut the front door so unceremoniously on him a short time before. Then he heard nothing more. He gazed around him as he sat with his hands tightly closed. Had it been only a dream? Naughty whined; Sardanapolis edged toward him and mechanically he began to brush him down until he shone as sleek and shining as his Assyrian namesake.

CHAPTER V

A CONTRETEMPS

More days passed and Mr. Heatherbloom continued to linger in his last position. It promised to be a record-making situation from the standpoint of longevity; he had never "lasted" at any one task so long before. Miss Van Rolsen, to his consternation, seemed to unbend somewhat before him, as if she were beginning - actually! - to be more prepossessed in his favor. These evidences that he was rising in the stern lady's good graces filled Mr. Heatherbloom with new dismay; destiny certainly seemed to be making a mock of him.

A week went by; two weeks - three, and still twice a day he continued to march to and from the park with his charges. The faces of all the nurse-maids and others who frequented the big parallelogram of green became familiar to him; he learned to know by sight the people who rode in the park and had a distant acquaintance with the squirrels.

He became, for the first time, aware one day, from the perusal of a certain newspaper he always purchased now, that the prince had returned to Russia. Although Miss Dalrymple refused to be interviewed, or to confirm or deny any statement, it was generally understood (convenient phrase!) that the wedding would take place in the fall at the old Van Rolsen home. The prince had left America in his yacht - the *Nevski* - for St. Petersburg, announced the society editor. After a special interview with the czar and a few necessary business arrangements, the nobleman would return at once for his bride. And, perhaps, he - Mr. Heatherbloom - would still be at his post of duty at the Van Rolsen house!

Since the day the prince had been with Miss Dalrymple in the conservatory, Mr. Heatherbloom had not seen, or rather heard, that gentleman at the house. But then he - Mr. Heatherbloom - belonged in the rear, and, no doubt, the prince had continued to be a daily, or twice, or three-times-a-day visitor to Miss Van Rolsen's elegant, if somewhat stiff, reception rooms. Now, however, he would come no more until he came finally to "take with him the bride -"

The thought was in Horatio's mind when for a third time he encountered her, face to face, on a landing, near a stair, or somewhere in the house, he couldn't afterward just exactly recall where, only that she looked through him, without recognition, speech or movement of an eyelash, as if he had been a thing of thin air! But a thing that became suddenly imbued with real life; inspired with purpose! She had permitted him to remain in the house, knowing his professed helplessness in the matter - she *must* have divined that - playing with him as a tigress with a victim (yes; a tigress! Mr. Heatherbloom wildly, on the spur of the moment, compared her in his mind to that fierce beautiful creature). He would force her to tell him to go; she would certainly not suffer him to remain there another day if he told her -

FREDERIC STEWART ISHAM

"Miss Dalrymple, there is something I ought to say. I could not help overhearing you and the prince, one day, several weeks ago, in the conservatory."

After he said it, he asked himself what excuse he had for saying it. If he had stopped to analyze the impulse, he would have seen how absurd, unreasonable and uncalled for his words were. But he had no time to analyze; like a diver who plunges suddenly, on some mad impulse, into a whirlpool, he had cast himself into the vortex.

She looked at him and there was nothing *in nubibus* to her about his presence now. The violet eyes saw a substance - such as it was; recognized a reality - of its kind! Before the clouds gathering in their depths, Mr. Heatherbloom felt inclined to excuse himself and go on; but instead, he waited. There was even a furtive smile on his lips that belied a quick throbbing in his breast; he thrust one hand as debonairly as possible into his trousers pocket. His attitude might have been interpreted to express indifference, recklessness, or one or more of the synonymous feelings. She thought so badly of him already that she couldn't think much worse, and -

"So," - had she been paler than her wont, or had excess of passion sent the color from her face? - "you are a spy as *well!*"

His head shot back a little at the accent on the "well", but he thrust his hand yet deeper into the pocket and strove not to lose that assumed expression of ease.

"I - a spy? I did not intend to - you - " He paused; if he wished to set himself right in her eyes, why should he have spoken at all? Mr. Heatherbloom saw he had not quite argued out this matter as he should have done; his bearing became less assured.

"Is there" - her voice low and tense - "anything despicable, mean, paltry enough that you are not?"

Mr. Heatherbloom moistened his lips; he strove to think of a reply, sufficiently comprehensive to cover all the features of the case, but not finding one at once apologetic and yet not so, remained silent. He made, however, a little gesture with his hand - the one that wasn't in the pocket. That seemed to imply something; he didn't quite know what.

She came slightly closer and his heart began to pound harder. A breath of perfume seemed to ascend between them; the arrows in her eyes darted into his. "How much - *what* did you hear?" she demanded.

"I - am really not sure -" Was it the orchids which perfumed the air? He had always heard they were odorless. The question intruded; his brain seemed capable of a dual capacity, or of a general incapacity of simultaneous considerations. He might possibly have stepped back a little now but there was a wall, the broad blank wall behind him. He wished he were that void she had first seemed to see - or not to see - in him. "I didn't hear very much - the first part, I imagine -"

"The first part?" Roses of anger burned on her cheek. "And afterward? - spy!" Her little hands were tight against her side.

He hesitated; her foot moved; all that was passionate, vibrant in her nature seemed concentrated on him.

"I don't think I caught much; but I heard him say something about fate, or destiny, and men coming into their own - that old Greek kind of talk, don't you know -" He spoke lightly. Why not? There was no need of being melodramatic. What had to be must be. He couldn't alter her, or what she would think. "Then - then I was too busy to catch more - that is, if I had wanted to - which I didn't!" He was forced to add the last; it burst from his lips with sudden passion; then they curved a little as if to ask excuse for a superfluity.

She continued to look at him, and he looked at her now, squarely; a strange calm descended upon him.

"And that," he said, "is all I heard, or knew, until this morning, when I saw in the paper," dreamily, "he was coming back in the fall for -"

The color concentrated with sudden swift brightness in her cheeks. "You saw that - any one - every one saw - Oh -"

She started to speak further, then bit her lip, while the lace stirred beneath the white throat. Mr. Heatherbloom had not followed what she said, was cognizant only of her anger. Her eyes were fastened on something beyond him, but returned soon, very soon.

"Oh," she said, "I might have known - if I let you stay, through pity, you would -"

"Pity!" said Mr. Heatherbloom.

"Because I did not want to turn you out into the street -"

She spoke the words fiercely. Mr. Heatherbloom seemed now quite impervious to stab or thrust.

"I permitted you to remain for" - she stopped - "remembering what you once were; who your people were! What" - flinging the words at him - "you might have been. Instead - of what you are!"

Mr. Heatherbloom gazed now without wincing; an unnatural absence of feeling seemed to have passed over his features, making them almost mask-like. It was as if he stood in some new pellucid atmosphere of his own.

"Of course," he said, as half speaking to himself, "I must have earned my salary, or Miss Van Rolsen wouldn't have retained me. So I am not a recipient of charity. Therefore," - did the word suggest far-away school-boy lessons on syllogisms and sophistries - "I have no right to feel offended in that you let me remain, you say, 'through pity', when as a matter of fact it was impossible for me to tender my resignation, in view of - " He finished the rest of a rather involved logical conclusion to himself, taking his hand out of his pocket now and passing it lightly, in a somewhat dragging fashion, over his eyes. Then he gazed momentarily beyond, as if he saw something appertaining to the "auld lang syne", but recalled himself with a start to the beautiful face, the threads of gold, the violet eyes.

"You will see to it now, of course" - his manner became brisk, almost businesslike - "that I, as a factor, am eliminated here? That, I may conclude, is your intention?"

"Perhaps," said the girl, a sibyl for intentness now, "you would prefer to go? To be asked to! You would find the streets" - with swift discerning contempt - "more profitable for your purpose than here, where you are known."

"Perhaps," assented Mr. Heatherbloom. He spoke quite airily; then suddenly stiffened.

At his words, the sight of him as he uttered them, she came abruptly yet nearer; her breath swept and seemed to scorch his cheek.

"I should think," she said, "you would be ashamed to live!"

"Ashamed?" he began; then stopped. There was no need of speaking further for she had gone.

CHAPTER VI

PLOT AND COUNTER-PLOT

Mr. Heatherbloom drifted; not "looking for a way", one was forced upon him. It came to him unexpectedly; chance served him. He would have thrust it from him but could not. During his more or less eccentric peregrinations in Central Park he had formed visual acquaintances with sundry folk; pictures of some of them were very dimly impressed on his consciousness, others - and the major part - on his subconsciousness.

Flat faces, big faces, red faces, pale faces! One countenance in the last class made itself a trifle more insistent than the others. Its possessor had watched with interest his progress, interrupted with entanglements, and had listened to the music of his march, the canine fantasia, staccato, affettuoso! Mr. Heatherbloom's halting footsteps in the park generally led him to the heights; it wasn't a very high point, but it was the highest he could find, and he could look off on something - a lake, or reservoir of water, he didn't know just which, and a jagged sky-line.

The person that exhibited casual curiosity in his movements and his coming thither was a woman. She seemed slight and sinuous, sitting there against the stone parapet, and deep dark eyes accentuated the

FREDERIC STEWART ISHAM

pallor of her face. He did not think it strange she should always be at this spot when he came; in fact, it was quite a while before he noticed the almost daily coincidence of their mutual presence at the same place, at about the same time. After her first half-sly, half-sedulous regard of him, she would look away; her face then wore a soft and melancholy expression; she appeared very sad.

It took quite a while for this fact to be communicated to Mr. Heatherbloom. Though she shifted her figure often, as if to call attention to the pale profile of her face against a leaden sky, his thoughts remained introspective. Only the sky-line seemed to interest him. But one day something white came dancing in the breeze to his feet. Absorbed in deep neutral tones afar, he did not see it; his four-footed charges, however, were quick to perceive the object.

"Oh!" said the lady.

Mr. Heatherbloom looked. "Is - is it yours?" he asked.

"It - was," she remarked with a slight accent on the last word.

He got up; there seemed little use endeavoring to rescue the handkerchief now.

"I'm afraid I've been rather slow," he remarked. "Quite stupid, I'm sure."

She may have had her own opinion but maintained a discreet silence. Mr. Heatherbloom stooped and gathered in the remnants. "You will permit me," he observed, "to replace it, of course."

"But it was not your fault."

"It was that of my charges, then."

"No; the wind. Let's blame it on the wind." She laughed, her dark eyes full on his, though Mr. Heatherbloom seemed hardly to see them.

After that when they met on this little elevation, she bowed to him and sometimes ventured a remark or two. He did not seem over-anxious to talk but he met her troubled face with calm and unvarying, though somewhat absent-minded courtesy. He replied to her questions perfunctorily, told her whom he served, betraying, however, in turn, no inquisitiveness concerning her. For him she was just some one who came and went, and incidentally interfered with his study of the sky-line.

By degrees she confided in him; as one so alone she was glad of almost any one to confide in. She wanted, indeed, needed badly, a situation as lady's maid or second maid. She had tried and tried for a position; unfortunately her recommendations were mostly foreign - from Milan, Moscow, Paris. People either scrutinized them suspiciously, or *mon Dieu*! couldn't read them. It was hard on her; she had had such a time! She, a Viennese, with all her experience in France, Italy, Russia, found herself at her wits' end in this golden America. Wasn't it odd, *tres drole?* She had laughed and laughed when she hadn't cried about it.

She had even tried singing in a little music-hall, a horribly common place, but her voice had failed her. Perhaps there was a vacancy at Miss Van - what was her name? There *was* a place vacant; the maid with the saucy nose, Mr. Heatherbloom indifferently vouch-safed, had just left to marry out of service.

"How fortunate!" the fair questioner cried; then sighed. Miss Van Rolsen, being a maiden lady, would probably be most particular about recommendations; that they should be of the home-made, intelligible brand, from people you could call up by telephone and interrogate. Had she been very particular in his case? Mr. Heatherbloom said "no" - not joyfully, and explained. Though she drew words from him, he talked to the sky-line. She listened; seemed thinking deeply.

"You are not pleased to be there?" Keenly.

"I? - Oh, of course!" Quickly.

She did not appear to note his changed manner. "This Miss Van Rolsen, - isn't she the one whose niece - Miss Elizabeth Dalrymple - recently refused the hand and heart of a Russian prince?" she said musingly.

"Refused?" he cried suddenly. "You mean -" He stopped; the words had been surprised from him.

"Accepted?" She looked at him closer. "Of course; I remember now seeing it in the paper; I was thinking of some one else. One of the other lords, dukes, or noblemen the town is so full of just now."

He got up rather suddenly, bowed and went. With narrowing eyes she watched him walk away, but when he had gone all melancholy disappeared from her face; she stretched herself and laughed. "*Voila!* Sonia Turgeinov, comedienne!"

Mr. Heatherbloom did not repair to the point of elevation the next day, nor the day after; but she met him the third day near the Seventy-second Street entrance. More than that, she insinuated herself at his side; at first rather to his discomfort. Later he forgot the constraint her presence occasioned him, when something she said caused him to look upon her with new favor. Beauty had momentarily escaped his vigilance and enjoyed a mad romp after a squirrel before she was captured.

What, his companion laughingly suggested, would have happened if Beauty had really escaped, and he, Mr. Heatherbloom, had been forced to return to the house without her? What? Mr. Heatherbloom started. He might lose his position, *n'est-cepas?* He did not answer.

The idea was born; why *not* lose Beauty? No, better still, Naughty; the prime favorite, Naughty. He looked into Naughty's eyes, and they seemed full of liquid reproach. Naughty had been his friend - supposititiously, and to abandon him now to the world, a cold place devoid of French lamb chops? A hard place for homeless dogs and men, alike! About to waive the temptation, Mr. Heatherbloom paused; the idea was capable of modification or expansion. Most ideas are.

But he shortly afterward dismissed the entire matter from his mind; it would, at best, be but a compromise, an evasion of the pact he had made with himself. It was not to be thought of. At this moment his companion swayed and Mr. Heatherbloom had just time to put out his arm; then helped her to a bench.

She partly recovered; it was nothing, she remarked

bravely. One gets sometimes a little faint when - it was the old, old story of privation and want that now fell with seeming reluctance from her lips. Mr. Heatherbloom had become all attention. More than that he seemed greatly distressed. A woman actually in need, starving - no use mincing words! - in Central Park, the playground of the most opulent metropolis of the world. It was monstrous; he tendered her his purse, with several weeks' pay in it. Her reply had a spirited ring; he felt abashed and returned the money to his pocket. She sat back with eyes half-closed; he saw now that her face looked drawn and paler than usual.

He, thought and thought; had he not himself found out how difficult it was to get a position, to procure employment without friends and helpers? He, a man, had walked in search of it, day after day and felt the griping pangs of hunger; had wished for night, and, later, wished for the morn, only to find both equally barren.

Suddenly he spoke - slowly, like a man stating a proposition he has argued carefully in his own mind. She listened, approved, while hope already transfigured her face. She would have thanked him profusely but he did not remain to hear her. In fact, he seemed hardly to see her now; his features had become once more reserved and introspective.

He reappeared at the Van Rolsen house that day without Naughty. Miss Van Rolsen, when she heard the news, burst into tears; then became furious. She was sure he had sold Naughty, winner of three blue ribbons, and "out of the contest" no end of times because superior to all competition!

A broken leash! Fiddlesticks! She penned advertisements wildly and summoned her niece. That young lady responded to protestations and questions with a slightly indifferent expression on her proud languid features. What did she think of it? She didn't really know; her manner said she really didn't care.

Mr. Heatherbloom, standing with the light of the window falling pensively upon him, she didn't seem to see at all; he had once more become a nullity. He rather preferred that role, however; perhaps he felt it was easier to impersonate annihilation, in the inception, than to have it, or a wish for it, thrust later too strongly upon him.

"I adhere to my opinion that he sold Naughty. I should never have employed this man," asserted Miss Van Rolsen, fastening her fiery eyes on Mr. Heatherbloom. "Why don't you speak, my dear, and give me your opinion?" To her niece.

"I haven't any, Aunt."

"You are discerning; you have judgment." Miss Van Rolsen spoke almost hysterically. "Remember he" - pointing a finger - "came without our knowing anything about him."

Miss Dalrymple did not stir; a bunch of bizarre-looking orchids on her gown moved to her even rhythmical breathing. "What was he? Who was he? Maybe, nothing more than -" She paused for want of breath, not of words, to characterize her opinion of Mr. Heatherbloom.

He readjusted his posture. It was very bright outdoors;

people went by briskly, full of life and importance; children whirled along on roller skates.

"When I asked your opinion, my dear, as to the wisdom of having employed this person in the first place, under the circumstances, why did you keep silent?" Was Miss Van Rolsen still talking, or rambling on to the impervious beautiful girl? "You should have called me foolish, eccentric; yes, that's what I was, to have taken him in as I did."

Miss Dalrymple raised her brows and moved to a piano to adjust the flowers in a vase; she smiled at them with soft enigmatic lips.

"If I may venture an opinion, Madam," observed Mr. Heatherbloom in a far-away voice, "I should say Naughty will surely return, or be returned."

"You venture an opinion!" said Miss Van Rolsen. "You!"

Miss Dalrymple breathed the fragrance of the flowers; she apparently liked it.

"You are discharged!" said Miss Van Rolsen violently to Mr. Heatherbloom. "I give you the two-weeks' notice agreed upon."

"I'll waive the notice," suggested the young man at the window quickly.

"You'll do nothing of the sort." Sharply. "It'll take me that time to find another incompetent keeper for them. And, meanwhile, you may be sure," grimly, "you will be very well watched."

"Under the circumstances, I should prefer - since you *have* discharged me - to leave at once."

"Your preferences are a matter of utter indifference. You were employed with a definite understanding in this regard."

Mr. Heatherbloom gazed rather wildly out of the window; two weeks. - that much longer! He was about to say he would not be well watched; he would take himself off - that she couldn't keep him; but paused. A contract was a contract, though orally made; she could hold him yet a little. But why did she wish to? He had not calculated upon this; he tried to think but could not. He looked from the elder to the younger woman. The latter did not look at him.

Miss Dalrymple had seated herself at the piano; her fingers - light as spirit touches - now swept the keys; a Debussey fantasy, almost as pianissimo as one could play it, vibrated around them. Outside the whir! whir! of the skates went on. A little girl tumbled. Mr. Heatherbloom regarded her; ribbons awry; fat legs in the air. The music continued.

"You may go," said a severe voice.

He aroused himself to belated action, but at the door he looked back. "I'm sure it will be all right," he repeated to Miss Van Rolsen. "On my word" - more impetuously.

At the piano some one laughed, and Mr. Heatherbloom went.

"Why on earth, Aunt, did you want to keep him two

weeks longer?" he heard the girl's now passionate tones ask as he walked away.

"For a number of reasons, my dear," came the response. "One, because he wanted to leave me in the lurch. Another - it will be easier to keep an eye on him until Naughty is returned, or" - her voice had the vindictive ring of a Roman matron's - "this person's culpability is proven. Naughty is a valuable dog and -"

Mr. Heatherbloom's footsteps hastened; he had caught quite enough, but as he disappeared to the rear, the dream chords on the piano, now louder, continued to follow him.

CHAPTER VII

DEVELOPMENTS

That night, as if his rest were not already sufficiently disturbed, a disconcerting possibility occurred abruptly to Mr. Heatherbloom. It was born in the darkness of the hour; he could not dispel it. What if the person in whom he had confided in the park were not all she seemed? He hated the insinuating suggestion but it insisted on creeping into his brain. He had once, not so long ago, in his search for cheap lodgings, stumbled upon a roomful of alleged cripples and maimed disreputables who made mendicancy a profession; their jibes and jests on the credulity of the public yet rang in his ears. What if she - his casual acquaintance of the day before - belonged to that yet greater class of dissemblers who ply their arts and simulations with more individualism and intelligence?

Mr. Heatherbloom sat up in bed. Naughty might be worth five or even ten thousand dollars. He remembered having read at some previous time about a certain canine whose proud mistress and owner was alleged to have refused twenty thousand for him. The perspiration broke out on Mr. Heatherbloom's face. Was Naughty of this category? He looked very "classy," as if there couldn't be another beast quite like him in the world. What had been the twenty-thousand-

FREDERIC STEWART ISHAM

dollar mistress' name; not Van - impossible!

But the more he told himself "impossible", the more positive grew a certain perverse inner asseveration that it was quite possible. And what if the person in the park had known it? He reviewed the circumstances of their different meetings; details that had not impressed themselves upon him at the time - that had almost escaped his notice, now stood out clearer - too clear, in his mind. He remembered how she had brightened astonishingly after the brief fainting spell when he had made his ill-advised proposal. It had been as elixir to her. He recalled how she had met him every day. Had it been mere chance? Or - disconcerting suspicion! - had she deliberately planned -

For Mr. Heatherbloom there was no sleep that night. At the first signs of dawn he was up and out, directing his steps toward the park, as a criminal returns to the haunts of his crime. No faces of any kind now greeted him there; only trees confronted him, gaunt, ghostlike in the early morning mists. Even the squirrels were yet abed in their miniature Swiss chalets in the air. The sun rose at last, red and threatening. He now met a police-man who looked at him questioningly. Mr. Heather-bloom greeted him with a blitheness at variance with his mood. Officialdom only growled and gazed after the young man as if to say: "We'll gather you in, yet."

It was past nine o'clock before Mr. Heatherbloom ventured to approach the house; as he did so, the front door closed; some one had been admitted. He himself went in through the area way; from above came joyous barks, a woman's voice; pandemonium. Mr. Heather-bloom listened. Later he learned what had happened; a young woman had brought back Naughty; a very honest young woman who refused all reward.

"Sure," said the cook, who had the story from the butler, "and she spoke loike a quane. 'I can take nothing for returning what doesn't belong to me, ma'am. I am but doing my jooty. But if ye plaze, would ye be lookin' over these recommends av mine - they're from furriners - and if yez be havin' ony friends who be wanting a maid and yez might be so good as to recommind me, I'd be thankin' of yez, for it's wurrk I wants.' Think av that now. Only wurrk! Who says there arn't honest servin' gurrls, nowadays? The mistress was that pleased with her morals an' her manners - so loidy-loike! - she gave her the job that shlip av a Jane had; wid an advance av salary on the sphot."

"You mean Miss Van Rolsen has actually engaged her?" Mr. Heatherbloom, face abeam, repeated.

"Phawt have I been saying just now?" Scornfully. "Sure, an' is it ears you have on your head?"

Mr. Heatherbloom, a weight lifted from his shoulders, departed from the kitchen. He had wronged her - this poor girl, or young woman, who, in her dire distress, had appealed to him. How he despised now the uncharitable dark thoughts of the night! How he could congratulate himself he had obeyed impulse, and not stopped to reason too closely, or to question too suspiciously, when he had decided to act the day before!

All is well that ends well. All he had to do now was to complete as unostentatiously as possible his term of service - But perhaps he would be released at once?

No; not at once! Those anxious to supersede him began to dribble in, it is true; but they faded away, one by one, after interviews with Miss Van Rolsen, and returned no more. They were a mournful lot, these would-be, ten-dollar-a-week custodians; Mr. Heatherbloom wondered if his own physiognomy in a general way would merge nicely in a composite photograph of them?

His duties he performed now as quietly as he could. Two weeks more, ten days, nine, eight! Then? Ah, then!

He did not see Miss Van Rolsen again nor Miss Dalrymple. He encountered the fair unknown, though, his acquaintance of the park, occasionally, as she in demure cap and white ruffled apron glided softly her allotted way. Sometimes he nodded to her in distant fashion, sometimes she got by before he actually realized he had passed her. She seemed to move so quickly and with such little ado; or, it may be, he was not very observant. He didn't feel very keen on mere minor details these days; he experienced principally the sensation of one who was now merely "marking time", as it were - figuratively performing a variety of goose-step, the way the German soldiers do.

But one day she - Marie, they called her - stopped him.

"I understand from one of the servants that it cost you your position to - do what you did. You know what I mean -"

He looked alarmed. "Don't worry about that."

"But shouldn't I?" Steady dark eyes upon him.

"On the contrary!" Vigorously.

"I don't understand - unless. -"

"The salary - it is nothing here" - Mr. Heatherbloom gestured airily. "I should do much better - one of my ability, you understand! - elsewhere."

"Could you?" She regarded him doubtfully. "But, perhaps, they - It was not very pleasant for you here, anyway. Miss Van Rolsen - her niece, Miss Dalrymple - does not like you." He started. "It was easy to see that; when I mentioned regretfully that the good fortune that brought me where there is plenty; to eat should have been the cause of your being in disfavor, she stopped me short." Mr. Heatherbloom studied the distance. "'The person you speak of intended leaving anyhow, ' she said, and her voice was - *mon Dieu*! - ice."

The listener swallowed. "Quite so," he said jauntily. "Miss Dalrymple is absolutely correct."

She regarded him an instant with sudden, very mature gaze. "I can't quite make you out."

"No one ever can. Don't try. It isn't worth while. Which reminds me" - he rattled on - "I did you an injury; an injustice -"

"Ah?" she said quickly.

"In my mind! You will excuse me, but do you know that night after I had consigned him to your care in the park, I afterward felt quite anxious -"

"For what?" She came closer.

"Wondering if you - Ha! ha!" Mr. Heatherbloom stopped; in his confusion, his endeavor to turn the conversation from himself and Miss Dalrymple, he seemed to be getting into deep waters.

"You wondered what?" In a low tone.

Since he now felt obliged to speak, he did, coolly enough. "If you had some ulterior motive!" he said with a quiet smile.

She it was who now started back, and her face paled slightly. "Why? - what ulterior motive? What do you mean?"

He told her in plain words. She breathed more evenly; then smiled sweetly. She had a strange face sometimes. "Thank you," she said. "You are very frank, *mon ami*. I like you none the less for it. Though you did so injure me - in your thoughts!" Her eyes had an enigmatic light. "Well, I must go now to Miss Dalrymple. She is beginning to be so fond of me." She drawled the last words as if she liked to linger on them. "You see I, too, have a little Russian blood in me." Mr. Heatherbloom looked down. "And I think she loves to hear me tell of that wonderful country - the white nights of St. Petersburg - the splendid steppes - the grandeur of our Venice of the north. Of course, she is immensely interested in Russia now." Significantly. "Its ostentation, its splendor, its barbaric picturesqueness! But tell me, what is her prince like? He is very handsome, naturally! Or she would not so dote on him!"

Mr. Heatherbloom's features had hardened; he did not

answer directly. "She likes to talk about Russia?" he said, half to himself.

Marie shrugged. "Is it not to be her country some day?"

"No, it isn't!" The words seemed forced from his lips; he spoke almost fiercely. "She may live there with him, but it will never be her country. This is her country. She is its product; an American to her finger-tips. And all the grand dukes and princes of the Winter Palace can't change her. She belongs to old California; she grew up among the orange trees and the flowers, and her heart will ever yearn for them in your frozen land of tyranny!"

"Oh! oh! oh!" said Mademoiselle Marie. "How eloquent monsieur can be! Quite an orator! One would say he, too, has known this land of orange trees and flowers!"

"I?" Mr. Heatherbloom bit his lip.

But she only shook a finger. "Oh! oh!" Altogether like a different person from his casual acquaintance of the park! He gazed at her closer; how quickly the marks of trouble, anxiety, had faded from her face; as if they had never existed.

"What do you mean?" he asked, looking into eyes now full of a new and peculiar understanding.

"Nothing," she said and vanished.

He gazed where she had been; he could not account for a sudden strange emotion, as if some one had trailed a shadow over him. A premonition of something going to happen; that could not be foreseen, or averted! Something worse than anything that had gone before! What nonsense! He pressed his lips tightly and went about his duties like an automaton.

Eight days - seven days - six days more! - only six -

CHAPTER VIII

THE UNEXPECTED

The blow fell, a thunderbolt from the clear sky. It dazed certain people at first; it was difficult to realize what had happened, or if anything *had* really happened. For might not what seemed a deep and dire mystery turn out to be nothing so very mysterious after all? A message would soon come; everything would then be "cleared up" and those most concerned would laugh at their apprehensions. But the hours went by, and the affair remained inexplicable; no word was heard concerning Miss Dalrymple's whereabouts; she seemed to have disappeared as completely as if she had vanished on the Persian magic carpet. What could it mean? The circumstances briefly were:

Miss Dalrymple, four or five days before Mr. Heatherbloom's term of service came to an end, had expressed a desire to revisit her old home and friends in the West. One of a party made up mostly of other Californians - now residents of New York city - the girl had failed to appear on the private car at the appointed time, and the train had pulled out, leaving her behind. At the first important stop a telegram had been handed to a gentleman of the party from Miss Dalrymple; it expressed her regret at having reached the station too late owing to circumstances she would explain later, and announced her intention of coming on, with her maid, in a few days. They were not to wait anywhere for her but to go right along.

The party did; it was sorry to have lost one of its most popular members but no one thought anything more of the matter until at Denver, after a telegram had been forwarded to the Van Rolsen house, in New York, asking just when Miss Dalrymple would arrive, as camping preparations for a joyous pilgrimage in the mountains were in progress.

Miss Van Rolsen gasped when this message reached her. Miss Dalrymple and her maid - a young woman newly engaged by Miss Van Rolsen - had left the house for the train to which the private car was attached; neither had been heard from since. The aunt had, of course, presumed her niece had gone as planned; she had received no word from her, but supposing she was of a light-hearted, heedless company thought nothing of that. It was possible Miss Dalrymple had actually missed her train; but if so, why had she not returned to her aunt's house?

Where had she gone? What had become of her? No trace of her could be found. Certain forces in the central railroad office at New York could not discover any evidence that the young girl had taken a subsequent train. There was no record of her name at any ticket office; no state-room had been reserved by, or for her; in fact, telegrams to officials in Chicago and other points west failed to elicit satisfactory information of any kind.

Miss Van Rolsen found herself with something real to worry about; she rose to the occasion; her niece, after all, was everything to her. The Van Rolsen millions were ultimately for her, and the old lady's every ambition was centered in the girl. She had been proud of her beauty, her social triumphs.

With great determination she set herself to solve the puzzling problem. Could people thus completely disappear nowadays? It seemed impossible, she asserted, sitting behind closed doors in her library, to the private agent of the secret-service bureau whom she had just "called in."

He begged to differ from her and pointed to a number of cases which had seemed just as strange and mysterious in the beginning. Ransom - the "Black Hand" - Who could say what secret influences had been at work in this case? It was a very important one; Miss Dalrymple had money of her own; she was known to be her aunt's heiress. The conclusion? - But this was not Morocco, or Turkey, Miss Van Rolsen somewhat vehemently returned.

True; we have had, however, our "civilized" Ransuilis, answered the agent and mentioned a number of names in support of his theory. No doubt, after an interval, Miss Van Rolsen would have news of her niece - through those who had perpetrated the outrage; or she might even receive a few written words from the girl herself. After that it was a question of negotiating, or, while professing to deal with the perpetrators, to ferret them out if one could. The latter course was dangerous, for those who stoop to this particular crime are usually of a desperate type; he and Miss Van Rolsen could consider that question later. Meanwhile she must avoid worry as much as possible. The young girl would, no doubt, be well treated.

Had the speaker looked around at this moment, he might have observed that the heavy curtains, drawn before the door leading into the hall and closed by Miss Van Rolsen, moved suddenly, but neither the agent nor Miss Van Rolsen, engrossed at the far end of the room, noticed. The drapery wavered a moment; then settled once more into its folds.

The telegram purporting to be from Miss Dalrymple to one of the party on the train, could - the agent went on - very easily have been sent by some one else; no doubt, had been. The miscreants had seized upon a lucky combination of circumstances; for two or three days, while Miss Dalrymple was supposed to be speeding across the continent, they, unsuspected and unmolested, would be afforded every opportunity to convey her to some remote and, for them, safe refuge. It was a cleverly planned coup, and could not have been conceived and consummated without - here he spoke slowly - inside assistance.

The curtain at the doorway again stirred.

"And now, Madam, we come to your servants," said the police agent. "I should like to know something about them."

"My servants, sir, are, for the most part, old and trusted."

"'For the most part'!" He caught at the phrase. "We will deal first with those who do *not* come in that category."

"There's a young man recently employed that I have not been at all pleased with. He leaves to-morrow."

"Ah!" said the visitor. "Not the person I met going out of the area way, with the dogs as I came in?"

She answered affirmatively.

"H - mn!" He paused. "But tell me why you have not been pleased with him, and, in brief, all the circumstances of his coming here."

Miss Van Rolsen did so in a voice she strove to make patient although she could not disguise its tremulousness, or the feverish anxiety that consumed her. She related the most trivial details, seeming irrelevances, but the visitor did not interrupt her. Instead, he studied carefully her face, pinched and worn; the angular figure, slightly bent; the fingers, nervously clasping and unclasping as she spoke. He watched her through habit; and still forbore speaking, even when she referred to the escape of her canine favorite from his caretaker and how the dog had later been returned, though the listener's eyes had, at this point, dilated slightly.

"After his carelessness in this matter, he seemed to want to get away from the house at once," observed Miss Van Rolsen, "without availing himself of the two-weeks' notice I had agreed to give him."

The visitor relapsed into his chair; an ironical light appeared in his eyes.

"Perhaps," added Miss Van Rolsen, "you attach no significance to the fact?"

"On the contrary, I attach every importance to it. Has it not occurred to you there was a little collusion in this

FREDERIC STEWART ISHAM

matter of the lost dog?"

"Collusion?" Miss Van Rolsen's accents expressed incredulity. "You must be wrong. Why, the young woman wouldn't even accept the reward. And it was not a small one!"

"Two hundred or so dollars, ma'am! Not her stake!" he murmured satirically. "I am afraid two hundred thousand dollars would be nearer the mark these people have set for themselves!"

"But she didn't ask for a place here; only for me to look over her references - one was from a lady I knew in Paris - and to recommend her to my friends - "

"She knew your other maid had left; this confederate had, of course, told her. It was all arranged that she should come here. Rest assured of that. And having accomplished her purpose - clever that she is! - she at once started to ingratiate herself with your niece, to make herself useful. As a mistress of languages she *was* useful, in fact more so than any ordinary maid. Where did she come from? Find out whom she represents, and - we'll have the key to the mystery. But she, too, has disappeared; after turning the game over to the others, perhaps. I would suggest cabling those foreign references this young woman gave you. They will, of course, including your Paris friend, know nothing of her; the name she gave you was not her own."

"But by what unfortunate combination of circum-stances" - Miss Van Rolsen spoke somewhat incohe-rently - "should these people have been led to settle on my niece as the victim of their cowardly designs?

There are so many others -"

"You forget the publicity concerning this prince your niece is to marry." The old lady stiffened. "Pardon my mentioning it, but Miss Dalrymple has in this connection been very much before the public gaze."

"Against her wish, sir, and mine!" snapped Miss Van Rolsen. "She - I - have both lamented the fact. But what can one do? The journalists settled on the prince as a fruitful source for speculation. He is of noble family, very wealthy, no fortune-hunter; which has made it all the more distressing for him and us." She seemed about to say something further; then her lips suddenly tightened. "As I say, it has been very distressing," she ended, after a pause. "I expect it was one of the reasons my niece wanted to get away from New York for a time."

"No doubt!" The caller's voice was courtesy itself although he probably but half-credited Miss Van Rolsen's protestations in the matter. People liked to complain of the press and newspaper notoriety, when in their hearts, perhaps, they were not so displeased to be in that terrible lime-light; especially when the person associated with them happened to be a count, or a duke, or a prince. "Unfortunately, one has to put up with these things," he now added. "But you are positive you have told me everything?"

An instant she seemed to hesitate. "I am positive you know everything relative to the subject."

He arose. "In that event" - his manner indicated a sudden resolution - "there is one little preliminary to be attended to."

"Which is -"

"To arrest this fellow, Heatherbloom!"

"Arrest? When?"

"At once! There is no time to be lost. Already -" He gave a sudden exclamation.

"What is it?" she asked.

He stepped toward the curtain; it moved perceptibly.

"Some one has been listening," exclaimed Miss Van Rolsen excitedly.

"Yes, some one." Significantly. As he spoke he threw back the curtain and revealed the door partly ajar.

"It must have been - Not one of my old servants - They would not have -"

He stopped her. "There's the front way out of this house and the area way below," he said rapidly. "Is there any other way of escaping to the street?"

"No."

He darted out of the room to the front door. She followed.

"Quite in time!" he said, casting a quick look both ways along the avenue and then letting his glance fall to the servants' entrance below.

"You think he will try to -"

He regarded her swiftly. "While I stand guard here, would you mind getting some one to 'phone my office and ask two or three of my men to step over at once? Not that I doubt my own ability to cope with the case" - fingering the handle of a weapon on his pocket - "only it is always well to take no chances. Especially now!"

"Now?"

"Since he has practically convicted himself and confirmed my theory. We shall get at the truth through him. We're nearer the solution of the matter than I dared hope for."

"I'll telephone myself!" she cried. And started back to do so when an excited face confronted her.

"If ye plase, ma'am!" It was the cook.

"What is it?" Miss Van Rolsen spoke sharply.

"If ye plase, I think, ma'am, this Mr. Heatherbloom has taken lave av his senses."

"Why, what has he been doing?"

"He has, faith, just jumped over the fence into our neighbor's yard on the corner, and -"

The man on the steps did not wait to hear more; with something that sounded like an imprecation he sprang quickly down to the sidewalk and ran toward the corner.

CHAPTER IX

WHO FIGHTS AND RUNS

As Mr. Heatherbloom prepared to issue from his neighbor's gate opening on the side street, the feminine voice of one of the servants in the rear of the corner house called out in alarm at sight of the strange figure speeding across their metropolitan imitation of a back yard. If anything were needed to stimulate the fugitive's footsteps, it was the sound of that voice. He stayed not on the order of his going, but pushing back the heavy bolt - fortunately his egress was not barred by a locked door - he tore open the gate and sprang to the sidewalk. Then without stopping, he ran on, away from the fashionable avenue. The street he traversed like many thoroughfares of its kind was comparatively deserted most of the time; nobody impeded his progress, though one or two people gazed after him from their windows.

He had gone about three-quarters of a block when the window spectators discerned a heavier built figure come lumbering around the corner, apparently in hot pursuit. Mr. Heatherbloom, glancing over his shoulder, also observed this person; his capture and subsequent incarceration seemed inevitable. Already the fugitive was drawing near to busier Fourth Avenue; there he would be obliged to relax his pace; he could not sprint down that thoroughfare without attracting undue attention. Behind, the pursuer called out; he was, however, too short of breath for compelling vocal effect.

Mr. Heatherbloom, on the contrary, had good control of his breathing and was, moreover, yet fresh and physically capable. Which fact made it the more difficult for him to settle down to a forced, albeit sharp walk as he approached the corner, when his gait suddenly accelerated once more.

A street-car had just started not very far from him and Mr. Heatherbloom ran after it. A fine pretext for speed was offered him; as he "let himself go" in the way he had once gone somewhere in the past in a hundred-yards' dash, he felt joyously conscious both of covering space quickly and that he did so without making himself particularly prominent. Fools who ran after street-cars were born every moment; he was happy to be relegated to that idiotic class by any onlookers. He caught the car while it was going; he didn't want it to stop for him.

Neither did it stop to pick up any one else for several blocks; there was a space before it unobstructed by traffic. The motorman turned on more power and Mr. Heatherbloom listened gratefully to the humming wheels. At the same time he looked back; at the corner where he had turned into Fourth avenue he fancied a number of people were gathering. He could surmise the cause; the stockily-built man - his pursuer - was asking questions; he had learned what had become of the fugitive and was presumably looking around for a "taxi." In vain. At least, Mr. Heatherbloom so concluded, because one did not appear in hot chase behind them.

The motorman still gave "rapid service"; the conductor looked at his watch, by which Mr. Heatherbloom imagined they had time to make up. He hoped so, then resented a pause at a corner for an old lady. How he wished she had not been afflicted with rheumatism, and could have got on without help! But at length the light-weight conductor did manage to pull the heavy-weight passenger aboard. Time lost, thirty seconds! The motorman manipulated the lever more deliberately now and they gathered headway slowly. Mr. Heatherbloom dared not remain longer where he was; as the car approached a corner near an elevated station, he got off. He was obliged to walk now a short distance but he did so hastily. Drawing near the iron steps, leading upward, he once more looked back; a "taxi" *was* whirling after him and he had no doubt as to its occupant. The street-car could easily have been kept in sight and his leaving it been noted.

Mr. Heatherbloom now threw discretion to the winds; dashing toward the stairway he ran up. Just as he reached the ticket window, the pursuing vehicle stopped below. Some one sprang out, did not pause to pay the chauffeur, but calling out to him his name, started after Mr. Heatherbloom. That gentleman had by this time boarded the train waiting above; he stood on the rear platform. Any moment the pursuer would appear. He did appear as the gates of the train were closed and the cars had started on their way.

Yet he did not give up for running alongside the last car he called out to the guard:

"Fugitive from justice! Criminal - on this train! Open

the gate for me!"

An instant the guard hesitated; rules, however, were rules.

"Five hundred dollars if you let me on!" the voice panted.

The guard in his own mind decided he would let the other on - too late; the last car dashed past the end of the platform. A faint sigh of relief from Mr. Heather- bloom was drowned in the tumult of the wheels; then he endeavored to appear indifferent, apathetic. It was not easy to do so; the secret-service agent had been heard by many others.

A "fugitive from justice" on the train! Mr. Heather- bloom tried to look as little the part as possible, to simulate by his expression a preoccupied young business man of heavy responsibilities. Fortunately the train was crowded; nevertheless he fancied people glanced especially at him. He wished now he were better dressed; good clothes may cover a multitude of sins. Still there was no reason why he should be suspected more than sundry other indifferently-dressed people. He would dismiss the thought, tell himself he was going down town on some little errand; he even devised what that errand should be - to procure theater tickets. But his brain did not seem quite capable of concentrating itself solely on desirable orchestra chairs; it constantly and perversely reverted to that other disagreeable subject - a "fugitive from -"

Whoever could the fellow be? He endeavored by a mental process to eliminate himself and see but a mythical some one else in a mythical background. A

FREDERIC STEWART ISHAM

short person; a tall one? What kind of person would the imaginary individual be, anyhow? And what had he done, what crime committed? Mr. Heatherbloom tried to think with the minds of all these other people on the train, to put himself figuratively in their shoes.

One young sprig of a girl, about fourteen, with sallow complexion and bead-like black eyes, kept regarding him. He conceived a profound dislike for her, shifted a foot; then straightened and banished her peremptorily from his environment. His principal interest lay now in casual glimpses of windows and speculation as to what was behind them. He varied this employment in a passing endeavor to decipher sundry signs that obtruded incidentally within range of vision.

He had made out only a few when the, train slackened and came to a standstill. Mr. Heatherbloom told himself he would get off as quickly as possible; then changed his mind and remained. People would, of course, argue that, under the circumstances, the unknown criminal would be among those to leave the train at the first opportunity.

A number got out; Mr. Heatherbloom noted the passengers who remained aboard and watched closely the departing ones. A few of the latter seemed slightly self-conscious, notably, an elderly spinster who, having never done anything wrong, was possessed of an unusual sensitiveness.

"See that slouchy chap - By jove, I believe -"

"Does look like a tough customer -"

"On the contrary, he just looks poor. "Mr.

Heatherbloom turned upon the two speakers warmly.

Why could he not have kept silent; why was he obliged to obtrude his opinion into their conversation?

They stared and he half turned as the train banged itself along once more. Where should he go? Reaching for a paper that some one had discarded, he sank into a vacant seat and opened the sheet with misgiving.

What would the big types say? Nothing! Miss Van Rolsen had managed to keep the strange affair of her niece's disappearance out of the columns of the papers. They knew nothing about it as yet - Only a single little item in the shipping news, in fine print, which suddenly caught his gaze bore in any way, and that a remote one, upon her niece and her affairs. Mr. Heatherbloom regarded it with dull glance. The few lines meant nothing to him - then; later he had cause to turn to them with abrupt wondering avidity. Now his eyes swept with simulated interest the general news of the day; he professed to read cable dispatches.

But an odd reaction seemed to have settled on him; the excitement of the chase became, for the moment, forgotten. The scope of his mental visuality no longer included the figure of the agent from the private detective bureau. An anxiety more poignant moved him; his thoughts centered on that other matter - the cause of Miss Van Rolsen's apprehensions - the while those emotions that had held him a listener behind the curtain in her library again stirred in his breast. He had not played the eavesdropper for any selfish purpose or through a sense of personal apprehension. The sudden realization of his own danger, had, perforce, awakened in him the need for quick action if he would save himself.

If? What chance had he? But for one compelling reason, one consuming purpose, he would not have fled at all; he would have faced them, instead! But he had work to do - he! A fugitive, a logical candidate for the prison cell! Ironical situation! Even now he heard a voice at his elbow.

"Mr. Heatherbloom!" Some one spoke suddenly to him and he wheeled with abrupt swift fierceness.

"Well, are you going to eat me up?" the voice laughed.

He looked into the pert face of Jane - the maid with the provoking nose - who had been at Miss Van Rolsen's. She had got on at the other end of the car at the last station, and after waiting a few moments for him to see her, had moved toward him, or a seat at his side just then vacated by some one preparing to leave. Mr. Heatherbloom's face cleared; he banished the belligerent expression.

"You look edible enough!" he said with forced jocularity.

"Indeed?" she retorted, surprised at such gallantry from one who had heretofore not deigned to pay her compliments. "I'll have to tell my husband about you." Playfully. "But how are things at Miss Van Rolsen's? Anything new?"

Mr. Heatherbloom murmured something about the customary routine; then, even as he spoke, became conscious of a sudden new disconcerting circumstance. The tracks for the up and the down trains on the elevated had widely separated and ran now on the extreme sides of the broad thoroughfare. From his side of the car the young man was afforded a view of the pavement below, between the two sustaining iron structures. A chill shot through him and his smile became set. Gazing down he discerned, on the street beneath and a little to one side of them, a motor-car, speeding fast, apparently bent on keeping up with them.

"How - how's your husband?" he said irrelevantly. The car *was* keeping up with them.

"Very well, thank you." (Would *it* reach the next station before them?)

"You - you have a pleasant home?" he asked. (A slight blockade below impeded, momentarily, the "taxi". Mr. Heatherbloom raised his handkerchief to his moist brow.)

"Lovely," she answered. "Are you going far?"

"Brooklyn," he said at random. What *were* they talking about? (The car was once more under way; fortunately their progress overhead would not be impeded by a press of vehicles.)

"That's where we live - Brooklyn," she said.

"Is it? Got a nice house?" He had practically asked this question before; but he hardly knew what he was saying. A policeman had stopped the "taxi" and was shaking his head, as at a rather "fishy" story. Mr. Heatherbloom by a species of telepathy, seemed to overhear the excited talk waging below.

"Oh, yes; lovely!" Jane's accents were but parenthetical to something else. The "taxi" had been allowed to proceed, in spite of the detaining thought-waves Mr. Heatherbloom had launched toward the officer of the law. The occupant had probably showed a badge; Mr. Heatherbloom stretched his neck out of the window.

"You can come around and see, sometime, if you want to." Pride in her voice. "And meet my husband." Husband was a very substantial baker.

"Charmed, I'm sure! Ha! ha!" He suddenly laughed.

"What is it?" She looked startled.

"Funniest accident!" He waved his hat, as at some one, out of the window. "See that taxi! Bumped into a dray. Ha! ha!"

"I don't see anything so funny in that." Straightening.

"No? You should have seen the expression on his face -"

"His? Whose?"

"The - ah, drayman's, of course! He - looked so mad."

"I should have thought," she observed, "the man in the car would have been the maddest It couldn't have hurt the dray much."

"No? Perhaps that's what made it seem so funny to me."

"Well," she said, "I never noticed before that you had a

great sense of humor."

"You never knew me." Jauntily.

They got off at Brooklyn Bridge together. As they made their way through the crowd, Mr. Heatherbloom appeared most care-free and very sedulous of his companion's welfare, especially when they passed one or two loiterers who seemed eying the passengers rather closely.

"Two for Brooklyn." Mr. Heatherbloom laid down a dime at the ticket office.

Soon, unmolested, he sped on once more; but as they crossed the busy river all his light-heartedness seemed suddenly to desert him; the questions he had been vainly asking himself earlier that day were reiterated in his brain. Where was she? What had become of her? His hands clasped closely. A red spot burned on his cheek.

CHAPTER X

A NEW-FOUND THEORY

"No; the prince isn't coming back to America , and she - Miss Dalrymple - isn't going to marry him!"

Jane's voice, running on rather at random, suddenly with unusual force penetrated Mr. Heatherbloom's consciousness.

"Not going - isn't - What are you talking about?" The young man's wavering attention focused itself on her now with swift completeness. He had hardly heard her, until a few moments before, when her conversation had first drifted to that ever fascinating feminine topic of foreign lords and American heiresses, then narrowed down, much to his inward disapproval, to one particular titled individual and one particular heiress "But you are mistaken, of course!" he said bruskly.

"Oh, am I?" she retorted. "I suppose you believe everything you read in the newspapers?"

Mr. Heatherbloom did not answer now; he was staring out of the window. Against the sky the jutting lines of buildings seemed to waver; new extraordinary angles and jogs seemed to assert themselves. His gaze had a glittering brightness when it turned. "Have you any better authority?"

His tone was a challenge. "I heard her tell him so myself," she said succinctly. "That she could never marry him and that he must never come back."

Mr. Heatherbloom's hand crumpled the newspaper; then mechanically he folded it and put it in his pocket. His look was once more bent outward; tiny specks, that were big steamboats going very fast, seemed motionless on the sparkling surface of the water afar. His thoughts scattered; he tried to collect them, to realize where he was, how he happened to be there; the identity of the speaker and what she had been saying! Certain preconceived, fixed ideas and conclusions had been toppled over, brushed aside in an instant. Was it possible?

"I was waiting to trim and fill the lamps," said Jane. (Miss Van Rolsen clung to oil lamps for reading.) "The prince and she were in the library. He has a loud voice, you know."

The young man did. "But why -"

"Search me!" Vivaciously. "He was the very pick of the whole cargo of dukes and the like. There isn't another girl in New York would have done it."

"But surely," scarcely hearing her last words, "no newspaper would dare to announce such a thing without -"

"Oh, wouldn't it? When it called up the house every day, almost, and got: 'There is nothing to say'? Didn't I answer the 'phone once or twice myself? 'Miss Van Rolsen declines to be interviewed concerning her niece. She has nothing to say.' I think I once giggled, the man's voice at the other end was so aggressive. He said he was the city editor himself. Is that very high up?"

Mr. Heatherbloom did not seem to hear. He scarcely saw his companion now; nevertheless, he was conscious of a desire to be alone, in order to concentrate, consider, reach for light and find it. But where could he discover a safe spot; his problem was a dual one; primarily, he must consider himself; he must not forget his own desperate situation and danger. The train, beginning to slacken, brought the sense of it once more poignantly to mind. His companion hadn't reached the station yet but he suddenly rose. The car stopped with a jerk; Mr. Heatherbloom murmured something hurriedly and dived for the door.

On the street he breathed deeply, standing as in a daze while the thunder of iron-rimmed wheels surrounded him. He was cognizant principally of certain words humming in his brain: The prince and she were not engaged! The nobleman not returning to America in the fall! Never coming back!

But that item in fine print in the newspaper he had in his pocket - what did it mean? Nothing, of course, beyond what it said; still -

Some one bumped into Mr. Heatherbloom; whereupon he suddenly realized that he was standing on one of the busiest corners and had been making himself as conspicuous as possible. Hastily he moved on. To what destination? He glanced toward a convenient saloon; it looked hospitable and inviting. Then he remembered they - man-hunters, in general - always searched the saloons first for criminals.

He started toward a side street but paused, reasoning that he was more prominent on comparatively isolated thoroughfares than on the swarming ones. A stream of women flowing into a big department store, exercised an odd attraction for him. Safety lay, perhaps, among numbers; at least, for the time, until he could devise a course of action. If he could conceive of one! If -

He must; he would. Every nerve in his body seemed to respond. Had he not embarked before this on desperate adventures; had he not fought in the face of over-whelming odds, and managed to hold his head up? A peculiar little smile played around the corner of his thin lips; it was like the flash of light on a blade. He joined the inflowing eddy.

Bargain day! He was crushed and crumpled but found himself ultimately on a stool in the rear of the store. No; he didn't want any marked-down collars or cuffs; he conveyed an impression to the solicitous clerk of some one waiting for some one. Patiently, uncomplai-ningly! With an unseeing eye for the hurrying and scurrying myriads! Time passed; he remained oblivious to the babble of voices. Timon in the wilderness, Diogenes in his tub, could not have been mentally more isolated from annoying human conso-ciation than was at the moment Mr. Heatherbloom, perched on a rickety stool amid a conglomeration of females struggling for lingerie.

Suddenly he stirred. "Have you a book department?" he asked an employee.

"Straight across; last aisle to the left."

Mr. Heatherbloom got up; his tread was slow; a som-nambulistic gleam appeared in his eye. Yet he was very much awake; he had never felt more keenly alert. He reached the book section.

Did they have any Russian fiction? Oh, yes; what kind did he want, nihilistic or psychological? *The Fire and Sword* kind, whatever that was; the second volume of the trilogy, if they had it in stock? Sure they had; but had he read the first volume? No; he didn't want that; he would begin in the middle of the trilogy. He always read trilogies that way.

The young lady in charge looked what she thought as she handed him the book. He paid her; unfortunately it cost more than the popular novels of the day. He rather gravely contemplated the few small bills he had left; the amount of his capital would not carry him very far, especially if unusual expenses should occur. Miss Van Rolsen still owed him a little money but he didn't see how he could collect that now.

Mr. Heatherbloom, armed with his book, sought a different part of the store - a small reception-room, where customers of both sexes were at liberty to read, write, or indulge in mental rest-cure, after bargain purchases. There he perused hurriedly, and by snatches, the volume; there was plenty of fire and plenty of sword in it; human passions bubbled and seethed. Suddenly he sat up straight and a suppressed exclamation fell from his lips; he closed the book sharply.

One or two old ladies looked at him but he did not see

them. His vision, clairvoyant-like, seemed to have lifted, to traverse broad seas, limitless steppes. His hands opened and closed, as if striving to reach and clutch something beyond flame of battle, scenes of rapine.

He got up dizzily. As he stepped once more into the street, the shadows had lengthened; twilight was falling. He stopped at a pawnbroker's, purchased a revolver and cartridges. He might need the weapon now more than ever. And money - he needed far more of that than he had. He spread in his palm the little wad of greenbacks he took from his pocket; counted them and a few silver pieces. Then seeking a ticket office, he made a few casual inquiries; a shadow rested on his countenance as he emerged from the place.

Next door to it a pile of gold pieces in a bank window shone mockingly before his eyes. So near - with only the plate-glass between him and the bright discs! Mechanically he began to count them, but suddenly turned from that profitless occupation and stood with his back to the window.

What availed resolution without dollars? His purpose might be strong, but poverty, a Brobdingnagian giant, laid its hand on his shoulder, crushing him down, holding him there, impotent, until the stocky man and his cohorts of the private detective office should come over and get him - to send him to the little island he had thought of when crossing the bridge to Brooklyn!

He fell back into a doorway. More money! - he must get it; must! He folded his arms tight over his breast. To think that this should be his one great, crying need - his!

FREDERIC STEWART ISHAM

Above, he heard footsteps descending the stairway at the foot of which he stood; Mr. Heatherbloom slipped out of the passage to the sidewalk and moved on. Chance took him back the way he had come; he had no choice of direction. Now he looked once more at the window of the pawnbroker, where he had stopped a short time before. He regarded the unredeemed pledges; seal-rings, watches, flutes, old violins; what not? If he only had something left; but all had gone - long ago.

All? He started slightly; considered; walked on. But he turned around, hesitatingly, and came slowly back. As he approached the door, his step grew more resolute. He walked briskly in. Without giving the proprietor time to come to the front of the shop, Mr. Heatherbloom moved at once to the back where the other sat behind his dusty glass cases.

"Here I am once more." He spoke with forced gaiety.

"What you want to buy now?"

"I don't want to buy anything; I want to sell something."

The pawnbroker's interest in the visitor at once departed.

"I have everythings! Everythings!" he grumbled. "Nearly every one wants to sell. I have no room for noddings more. Good night!"

"But I've something special," said Mr. Heatherbloom. As he spoke he took from an inner pocket a little parcel in pink tissue-paper; he fingered it a moment, removing an ivory miniature from a frame, passed the paper quickly about the picture once more, and returned it to his pocket. Then he handed the frame, over the case, to the pawnbroker. "What do you think of that, my Christian friend?" he said with a show of jocularity that didn't ring quite true.

The pawnbroker bent his dull face close to the article; it was gold. A pretty trinket, set with a number of brilliants, it might have come from the Rue Royale or the Rue de la Paix.

"Cost about five hundred francs," observed Mr. Heatherbloom, watching the other closely. "One hundred dollars, without the duty."

"Where'd you get it?"

"None of your business." With a smile.

The man moved toward a telephone at his back. "Do you know what I'm going to do?"

"I am curious."

"'Phone the police."

"Is that an invitation for me to depart? If so -" Mr. Heatherbloom reached for the little gold frame.

"Oh, no," said the man, retaining the graceful article. "The police will find out who this belongs to."

"Tut! tut!" observed Mr. Heatherbloom lightly. Something on the edge of the showcase pointed over it; the hand the proprietor professed to raise toward the telephone fell to his side; he seemed about to call out. "Don't!" said the visitor. "It's loaded; you saw me put in the cartridges yourself. Your little game is very passe; I had it worked on me once before, and placed you in your class - a fourth-rater, with a crib for loot!"

The other considered; this customer's manner was ominously quiet and easy; he didn't like it. A telepathic message that flashed from the gleaming gaze above the shining tube suggested an utterly frivolous indifference to tragic consequences. The proprietor moved away from the telephone.

"Fifteen dollars," he said.

"Twenty," breathed Mr. Heatherbloom insinuatingly.

The man put his hand in his pocket and counted out the money. The caller took it, said something in those same blithe significant accents about what would happen if the other made a move in the next two or three minutes, then vanished from the store. He did not keep to the busy thoroughfare now, but shot into a side street. Would the pawnbroker hide the frame and then call the police? It was quite possible he might thus seek to get into their good graces and revenge himself at the same time. Mr. Heatherbloom turned from dark byway to dark byway. He knew there was a possibility that he might keep going throughout the night without being taken; but what would he attain by so doing, how would that profit him?

He had to get back to New York at once, and as speedily as possible! The shining face of a street clock that a short time before he had looked at, admonished him there were no moments to spare, if he would carry out his plan, his headstrong purpose - to verify or disprove a certain wild theory - which would take him where, lead to what? No matter! Above, between black shadows of tall buildings, he saw a star, bright, beautiful. Something in him seemed to leap up to it - to that light as frostily clear as her eyes! A taxi passed; he hailed it.

"How much to Jersey City?" he asked in feverish tones.

The man approximated a figure; it was large, but Mr. Heatherbloom at once got in.

"All right," he said. "Only let her go! I've a train to catch."

"You don't want to land us in the police court, do you?" asked the chauffeur.

Mr. Heatherbloom devoutly hoped not.

CHAPTER XI

MISCALCULATIONS

Two days later, on a bright afternoon, a young man stood on the edge of a sea-wall called the Battery. It was not *the* Battery, commanding a view of the out-going and incoming maritime traffic of the continent's metropolis, but another Battery, overlooking another harbor, or estuary, landlocked save for an entrance about a mile in width. Behind him lay, not a great, but a little, city; hardly more than a big town; before him a few vessels of moderate tonnage placidly plied the main or swash channels.

The scene was tranquilizing; nevertheless the young man appeared out of harmony with it. His face wore a feverish flush; his eyes had a restless gleam. He had only a short time before come to town, entering in unconventional fashion. As the train had slackened at a siding on the outskirts he had quietly, and unperceived, slipped off the back platform of the rear car; then made his way by devious and little frequented side streets to the sea-front.

There, his eager gaze scanned the craft, moving in the open, or motionless at the distant wharfs. An expression of acute disappointment passed over his features; his eyes did not find what they sought. Had that mad flight been for nothing? Had he but run into a new kind of "pocket" here, all to no purpose?

Mr. Heatherbloom sat down; he was weary and worn. The dancing sparkles laughed at him; he did not feel like "laughing back". Even as he leaned against the parapet a newsboy close at hand called out:

"All about the mysterious abduction! One of the miscreants traced to this city! Superintendent of police warned of his probable arrival!"

The lad looked at Mr. Heatherbloom as he shouted; that gentleman returned his gaze with unflinching stolidness.

"What abduction?" he asked.

"Beautiful New York heiress."

The voice passed on; the fugitive was once more alone with his thoughts. If they had been wild, turbulent before, what were they now? His hands closed; at the moment he did not bemoan his own probable fate, only the fact that the clue bringing him here had been false - false!

Another voice - this time a man's - accosted him. Mr. Heatherbloom sprang swiftly to his feet but the person, an old darky, did not appear very formidable.

"Got a match, boss?" he inquired mildly.

Mr. Heatherbloom's bright suspicious glance shot into the good-humored, open look of the other; that person's manner betrayed no ulterior motive. Perhaps he had not yet heard the newsboy; did not know - Mechanically the young man answered that he did not possess the article required, but the intruder still lingered; he had accosted the other partly because of a desire for desultory conversation. Mr. Heatherbloom, after a moment's careful scrutiny, showed a disposition to be accommodating in this regard; he even took the initiative - suddenly, asking question after question about this boat and that. Her name; when she had come; where she was going; of what her cargo consisted? The other replied willingly. Like many of his kind in the port, although he could not read or write, he was wise in harbor-front knowledge, knew all the floating tramps and the sailing craft.

"I suppose it's always about the same old boats drop in here?" Mr. Heatherbloom, after a little, observed insinuatingly.

"Yes, always de same ole tubs," assented the darky.

A shadow crossed the other's face, but he managed to assume a light air. "Battered hulks and sailing brigs of a past generation, eh?" He put the case strongly, but the darky only nodded smilingly. His strong point in conversation was in agreeing with people; he even forgot patriotism toward his own port in being amiable.

Mr. Heatherbloom glanced now beyond them to the right and the left; but no one whom he had reason to fear came within scope of his vision. His figure relaxed. When would they come to take him? The newsboy's words reiterated themselves in his mind. "Traced to this city!" Of course; Miss Van Rolsen's millions were at the command of the secret-service bureau; his description had been telegraphed far and wide. And when it should be fruitful of results, what would become of his theory? Nevertheless, he would go on, while he could, to the last.

If he tried to explain they would consider it but a paltry blind to cover his own criminality. He could expect no help from them; he had to triumph or fail through his own efforts. To fail, certainly; it was decreed.

For the moment something in his breast pocket seemed to burn there, a tiny object, now without the frame. Involuntarily he raised his hand; then his figure swayed; the street waved up and down. He had eaten little during the last two or three days. Scornfully in his own mind he berated that momentary weakness and steadied himself. His eyes, cold and clear, now returned to the colored man; he groped for and took up the thread of the talk where he had left it.

"Old hulks and brigs! You don't ever happen to have any really fine boats come in here, do you? Like Mr. Morgan's big private yacht, for example?"

"No; we ain't never seen dat craft yere. Dis port's more for lumber and -"

Mr. Heatherbloom looked down. "I saw an item in the paper" - he strove to speak unconcernedly - "a Marco-nigram - that a certain Russian prince's private yacht - the *Nevski* - had damaged her propeller, or some other part of her gear, and was being towed into this harbor for emergency repairs."

"Oh, yes, boss!" said the man. The listener took a firmer grip on the parapet. "You done mean de big white boat w'at lies on de odder side ob de island; can't see her from yere. Dey done fix her up mighty quick an' she gwine ter lebe to-night."

"Leave to-night!" Mr. Heatherbloom's face changed; suppressed eagerness, expectancy shone from his eyes; he turned away to conceal it from the other. "Looks like good fishing over there near the island," he observed after a pause.

"Tain't so much for fishin' as crabbin'," returned the other.

"Crabbing!" repeated Mr. Heatherbloom. "A grand sport! Now if - are you a crabber?" The darky confessed that crabbing was his main occupation; his boat swung right over there; for a dollar he would give the other several hours' diversion.

Mr. Heatherbloom accepted the offer with alacrity. A few moments later, seated in a dilapidated cockle-shell, he found himself slamming over the water. The boat didn't ship the tops of many seas but it took in enough spray over the port bow to drench pretty thoroughly the passenger. In the stern, the darky handling the sheet of a small, much patched sail, kept himself comparatively dry. But Mr. Heatherbloom didn't seem to mind the drenching; though the briny drops stung his cheek, his face continued ever bent forward, toward a point of land to the right of which lay the island that came ever nearer, but slowly - so slowly!

He could see the top of the spars of a vessel now over the high sand-hills; his body bent toward it; in his eyes shone a steely light. Their little boat drew closer to the near side of the island; the hillocks stood up higher; the tapering topmasts of the craft on the other side disappeared. The crabber's cockle-shell came to anchor in a tranquil sandy cove.

Mr. Heatherbloom, although inwardly chafing, felt obliged to restrain impatience; he could not afford to awaken the darky's suspicions, therefore he simulated interest and - "crabbed". He enjoyed a streak of good luck, but his artificial enthusiasm soon waned. He at length suggested trying the other side of the island, whereupon his pilot expostulated.

What more did his passenger want? The latter thought he would stretch his legs a bit on the shore; it made him stiff to sit still so long. He would get out and walk around - he had a predilection for deserted islands. While he was gratifying his fancy the darky could return to his more remunerative business of gathering in the denizens of the deep.

Five minutes later Mr. Heatherbloom stood on the sandy beach; he started as if to walk around the island but had not gone far before he turned and moved at a right angle up over the sand-hill. The dull-hued bushes that somehow found nourishment on the yellow mound now concealed his figure from the boatman; the same hardy vegetation afforded him a shelter from the too inquisitive gaze of any persons on the yacht when he had gained the summit of the sands.

There, he peered through the leaves down upon a beautiful vessel. She lay near the shore; whatever her injury, it seemed to have been repaired by this time for few signs of life were apparent on or about her. Steam was up; a faint dun-colored smoke swept, pennon-like, from her white funnels. Some one was inspecting her stern from a platform swung over the rail, and to Mr.

FREDERIC STEWART ISHAM

Heatherbloom's strained vision this person's interest, or concern, centered in the mechanism of her rudder. The trouble had been there no doubt, and if so, the yacht had probably come, or been brought near the island at high water, and at low tide any damage she might have suffered had been attended to. Her injury must have been more vexatious than serious. Would she, as the darky had affirmed, leave when the tide was once more at its full? Her lying in the outer, instead of in the inner harbor, seemed significant. Time passed; the person on the platform regained the deck and disappeared. In the bushes the watcher suddenly started.

Something at one of the port windows had caught his glance. A ribbon? A fluttering bit of lace? A woman's features that phantom-like had come and vanished? He looked hard - so steadily that spots began to dance before his sight, but he could not verify that first impression. Yet he remained. The shadows on the furze grew longer, falling in strange angular shapes down the hillside; the sun dipped low. At length Mr. Heatherbloom, after the manner of one who had made up his mind to something, abruptly rose.

He walked back toward the cove where he had disembarked. As he drew near the darky caught sight of him, pulled up "anchor" and paddled his boat to the shore. But Mr. Heatherbloom did not at once get in; his eyes rested on the bushel or so of freshly caught, bubble-blowing crabs. He strove to appear calm and matter-of-fact.

"What do you expect to get for them?" he asked, pointing.

"'Bout fifty cents de dozen, boss. Crab market ain't

what it ought ter be jest now."

"Why don't you try to sell them to the yacht over there?" Mr. Heatherbloom managed to speak carelessly but it was a difficult task.

"Jest becos she is 'over there', boss," returned the darky lazily. "Mighty swift tide sweeping around de head of dat island!" he explained.

"And you don't like rowing against it?" Quickly. "See here, I'll tell you what I'll do. I like a bit of exercise, and just for the gamble, I'll give you sixty cents a dozen for the lot, and keep all I can get over that. The owner of that craft is a Russian and all Russians like sea food. When they can't get caviar, they'll no doubt make a bid for crabs."

"Dat sounds like berry good argumentation, boss. Make it seventy" - avarice struggling on the dusky countenance - "an' -"

"Done!" said Mr. Heatherbloom, endeavoring to disguise the fierce eagerness welling within him. "Here's on account!" Tossing his last bill to the other. "And now, get out. It'll be easier pulling without you."

The darky grinned and obeyed. This was a strenuous passenger truly, not averse to stiff rowing, after a stiff walk, "jest for pleasure". But the dusky pilot had met these anomalous white beings before - "spo'tsmen", they called themselves. And a certain sense of humor, as Mr. Heatherbloom sat down to the oars, caused the colored man involuntarily to hum: *I'se got a white man a-workin' for me.* He had only finished a bar or two, however, when the tune abruptly ceased on his lips.

"Dat's too bad," he said. "I guess de deal's off, boss." Regretfully.

"Eh?" Mr. Heatherbloom looked around. He meant to keep the man to his bargain now, by force if necessary.

"Look dar!" continued the darky.

Mr. Heatherbloom did look in the direction indicated. A puff of black smoke could be seen rising over the island, and - significant fact! - the dark smudge seemed to be crawling along beyond the sky-line of the sand-hill. The young man turned pale.

"It's de Russian yacht, boss. She's under way all right!"

Mr. Heatherbloom continued to gaze. Where the island was lower he saw the topmasts moving along - then the boat herself, white, beautiful, swinging out from behind, with bow pointed seaward and steaming fast.

"Dat's too bad," murmured the colored man. "I done be powerful disappointed, boss!"

The other did not answer. Going! going! He had waited too long to board her. He could not reach her now - he would never reach her. The flame of the dying sun flared in Mr. Heatherbloom's face, but he continued motionless.

CHAPTER XII

ON THE ROAD

Gone! It was the only word he, could think of. Every thought, every emotion centered around it. He could not reason or argue. No plan occurred to him now. He continued to sit still, seeing but one picture - a boat vanishing. Night had begun to fall as they returned to the city. Its lights played mockingly in the darkness. Mr. Heatherbloom viewed them with apathetic gaze. The secret-service man, the chief of police and his assistants were on shore somewhere waiting to capture him, but he did not care. Let them take him now! What did it matter?

When the boat reached land he got out like an automaton. Perhaps he made answer to the darky's last cheerful good night, but if so he spoke without knowing it. The boatman let him go, willingly; Mr. Heatherbloom hadn't asked for his last bill back again and the other overlooked reminding him of his remissness. The greenback was considerably more than the fare.

Indifferent to his fate, Mr. Heatherbloom moved on; no one molested him. He walked along dark highways, not through fear of being apprehended, but because his mood was dark. He did not even notice where he went;

FREDERIC STEWART ISHAM

he just kept going. He forgot he was hungry, but at length, as in a dream, he began to realize a physical weariness. Overwrought nature asserted itself; he was not made of iron; his muscles responded reluctantly. Without observing his surroundings, he sank listlessly to the earth; the cool grass received his exhausted frame. Beyond, some distance away, the lights of the city threw now a sullen glow on the sky. All was comparatively still about him; the noise of the city was replaced by the lighter sound of vehicles on the well kept, almost non-resounding country road. It seemed to be a main thoroughfare, but with little life and animation about it at that evening hour. A buggy did go by occasionally, however, and, not far from Mr. Heatherbloom, at a curb, stood a motor-car.

He had suffered himself to relax on the ground in front of a small house set well back among spectral-looking trees and surrounded by a stone wall overgrown with foliage. Mr. Heatherbloom remained unmindful of his surroundings. The lamps of the car near by were not lighted; a single figure on the front seat was barely distinguishable. Now this person got down and lighted a cigarette; he seemed restless, walked to and fro, and glanced once or twice at the house. From a single window a faint light gleamed; then it vanished, only to reappear a few moments later at another window. Among the masses of foliage fireflies glistened; a tree-toad began to make a sound but almost immediately stopped. The front door had apparently opened and some person or persons came out. The faint crunchings on the gravel indicated more than one person. Now they stepped on the grass, for there were no audible indications of their approach. The man near the machine threw quickly away his cigarette and opened the door of the car. Several people, issuing from the gate, crossed the sidewalk and got in. Mr. Heatherbloom was hardly aware of the fact; they seemed but unmeaning shadows.

The driver bent over and lighted one of his lamps. As he did so, the flare revealed for an instant his face - square, rather handsome and bearded. A faint flicker of interest, for some reason undefinable to himself at the moment, swept over Mr. Heatherbloom. He had been lying where the grass was tall and now raised himself on his elbow, the better to peer over the waving tops. The car had gathered headway and swung out into the road, when suddenly some one in it laughed and uttered an exclamation in a foreign tongue. That musical note - a word he did not understand - was wafted to Mr. Heatherbloom. It acted upon him like a galvanic shock; he sprang to his feet and, bewildered, stared after the machine. What had happened; was he dreaming? He could hardly at first believe the evidence of his senses, for the laugh, coming back to him in the night, was that of the woman for whom he had procured employment at Miss Van Rolsen's. He could have sworn to the fact now. And the man whose countenance he had so briefly seen was, no doubt, of her own nationality - a Russian!

Involuntarily, without realizing what he did, Mr. Heatherbloom started to run in the direction the car had gone, but he soon stopped. What madness! - to attempt to catch a sixty-horse-power machine! Why, it was nearly a mile away already. The young man stood stock-still while a cogent reaction swept over him. The woman had passed within fifty feet of where he had lain, head near the earth, moping. A mocking desire to atone for a great remissness found him impotent. There seemed nothing for him to do now but to reconcile himself to the irreconcilable, to stay here, while every desire urged him to follow her, to learn why this woman was in the car and who was with her. Naturally, he had expected she would be on the yacht now steaming away out to sea, and here she was. A new enigma confronted him.

Mr. Heatherbloom continued to stand in the center of the road. His head whirled; he panted hard, out of breath from his recent dash. A loud honk! honk! from another machine coming unexpectedly up behind, caused him to leap aside just in time. The second car whizzed by, although obeying an impulse born on the instant, he called out wildly, waving his arms to bring it to a halt. If they saw his strange motions - which was unlikely, the night being dark - they did not heed them. Soon the second machine was some distance away; then its rear light gleamed like a vanishing coal and suddenly disappeared altogether around a bend of the road.

He looked back; no other vehicle of any description was in sight now. But it profited nothing to continue passive, immovable. He had to act, to walk on, no matter how slowly; his face, at least, was set in the direction the woman had gone. How long it took him to reach the turn of the thoroughfare he could not tell, but at length there, he came again to an abrupt stop. Some distance ahead in the road appeared a machine, motionless - waiting, or broken down.

Which car was it? The one containing the woman, or the other that came after? If the former - He pressed on eagerly, yet keeping to the shadows, alive once more to the need of caution. His heart pounded hard; he could see a form passing in front of the machine; the light of the lamp enabled him now to make out the other occupants - three men. No woman was with them. This became poignantly, irrefutably evident as he drew nearer. He could see plainly the empty car and the trio of figures; he could hear them talking but was not yet able to distinguish what they said. These were the people whose attention he had tried to attract back there in the road. His purpose then, occurring to him in a flash, renewed itself strongly now. He would ask their aid; circumstances might enable him to do so now with better grace. He had had a good deal of experience with cars of divers kinds and makes at different times in the past. Why not proffer these strangers his fairly expert services? He felt sure he could soon learn, and repair, what was wrong with the machine. Having made himself useful, he could then intimate that a "lift" down the road would be acceptable. And he would probably get it.

But he did not carry out his intention. Something he heard as he came closer to them caused him to hesitate and reconsider. Mixed with anathemas directed against the car, of rather a cheap type, were words that had for him more than passing significance. These men were after some one, and that the some one was none other than himself, Mr. Heatherbloom soon became fully convinced. Fate had been kinder to him than he knew when he had endeavored, and failed, to win their notice. He crouched back now against a rail fence; their low disgruntled tones were still borne to him. For some moments they continued to work over the machine without apparently being able to set it to rights.

"If this goes on much longer," said one of them, "he'll get away from Brownville."

"Providin' he's there!" grumbled another. "People are always seeing an escaped criminal in a dozen different localities at the same time."

Brownville! The listener soon divined, from a sentence dropped here and there, that the place was a little fishing village a short distance down the coast. He surmised, also, that they had by this time the main harbor of the city fairly watched as far as outgoing vessels were concerned, and were reaching out to prevent a possible exit from the smaller community. Fishing craft leaving from there could easily take out a fugitive and thus enable him to escape. This contingency the authorities were now endeavoring to avert; that they also had some kind of a clue, pointing to their present destination and inciting them to make haste thither, was evident from the skeptical remark Mr. Heatherbloom had overheard.

A series of explosions, as sudden as spasmodic, broke in on the listener's thoughts. "Hurray!" said one. "We're off!"

And they were, quickly. Mr. Heatherbloom also moved with extreme abruptness and expedition. Waiting in the shadow until they had all sprung into the car and the machine had fairly started, he then darted forward, seized a strap and clinging as best he might, hoisted himself to the place in the rear designed for a trunk. One desire only, in resorting to this expedient, moved him - to get in touch as soon as possible, if possible, with the other car. This machine, of inferior build, suggested, it is true, a dubious way to that end but it was the best that offered.

He did not see the incongruity of his position, of being

a passenger, though secretly and surreptitiously, of the car containing those embarked on a mission so closely concerning himself. Instead of fleeing from them he was actually courting their company, pursuing himself, as it were! At another time he might have smiled; now the situation had for him nothing of the comic; it was tragically grim, also decidedly unpleasant. A strong odor of gasolene permeated his nostrils until he was nearly suffocated by it and all the dust, stirred by their flight, swirled up on him, making it difficult to refrain from coughing. Fortunately the machine had a monopoly on noises, and any sound from him would have passed unnoticed. He had ridden the "bumpers" not so long ago on freights, and, perforce, indulged in kindred uncomfortable methods of free transportation in the course of his recent career, but he had never experienced anything quite so little to be desired as this.

The driver had begun to speed; as if to make up for lost time, he was forcing the engine to its limit. The machine, of light construction, shook violently, negotiated the steep places with jumps and slid down on the other side with breakneck velocity. The dust thickened about Mr. Heatherbloom's head so that he could scarcely see. His arms ached and every bump nearly tore him loose. He wound the strap around his wrist and strove to ensconce himself deeper in a place not large enough for him. He was on an edge all the time, and felt as if he were falling over every moment; the edge, too, was sharp and dug into him.

Mr. Heatherbloom, however, had little thought of bodily discomfort; he was more concerned in making progress and the difficulty of maintaining his position. His only fear was that he would be compelled to abandon his place because his physical energy might not be equal to the demands put upon it. He set his teeth now and began to count the seconds. The faster they went, the better was his purpose served; he strove to find encouragement in the thought. The other car could make a superior showing in the way of speed, but it might stop voluntarily somewhere after a while, or something might happen to arrest its progress. The race did not always belong to the swift. He endeavored to formulate some plan as to just what he would do if he did finally manage to overtake the woman and her party, but at length ceased trying. Sufficient unto the moment were the problems thereof; he could but strive in the present. He dispelled the fear that he could not hold on much longer, and filled himself with new determination not to yield. But even as he did so, a bigger bump than any they had yet encountered jerked him abruptly from his place.

When finally he managed to collect himself and his senses and sit up uncertainly in the road, the car was far away. The snap of exploding gasolene grew faint - fainter - then ceased altogether.

CHAPTER XIII

IN THE NIGHT

A wayworn figure, some time thereafter, moved slowly along the deserted road, where it ran like a winding ribbon over the top of a great bluff. A sea wind, coming in varying gusts, bent low the long grass and rustled in the bushes. The moon had escaped from behind dark clouds in a stormy sky and threw its rays far and wide. They imparted a frosty sheen to the wavy surface between road and sea and brightened the thoroughfare, which, lengthening tortuously, disappeared beneath in a tangle of forest or underbrush.

Mr. Heatherbloom gazed wearily down the road, then over the grass. In the latter direction, afar, a strip of ocean lay like an argent stream flowing between the top of the bank and the horizon. Toward that illusory river he, leaving the main highway, walked in somewhat discouraged fashion. It might avail him little, so much time had elapsed, but from the edge of the bluff he would be afforded a view of the surrounding country and the topography of the coast.

A vast spread of the ocean unfolded to his gaze before he had reached the brink of the prominence. His heavy-lidded eyes, sweeping to the right, rested on a heterogeneous group of dwellings scattered well above

FREDERIC STEWART ISHAM

the sands and directly below a wooded uprising of land. Myriad specks of light glimmered amid shadowy roofs. Brownville? Undoubtedly! A board walk ran along the ocean and a small pier extended like an arm over the water. On the faintly glistening sands old boats, drawn up here and there, resembled so many black footprints.

Not far from where Mr. Heatherbloom stood a path went downward, a shorter way to the village than by the road he had just left. He stared unthinkingly a moment at the narrow walk; then began mechanically to descend. A dull realization weighed on him that when he reached his destination the woman would be far away. He wondered why he had gone on, under the circumstances - why he had ever thought he stood a ghost of a chance of overtaking her? Only the hopelessness of the situation, in all its grim verity, faced him now.

The path zigzagged through the bushes. At a turn the village was lost to sight; in front was a sheer fall to the sea. As he kept on, projecting branches struck him and raising his hand to guard his face, he, tripped and almost fell. Recovering himself, he glanced down; something had caught on his shoe and he leaned over to loosen it. His fingers closed on a long strip of soft substance - a veil, the kind worn by women motoring! Mr. Heatherbloom's eyes rested on it apathetically, then with a sudden flash of interest; a faint but heavy perfume emanated from the silky filament. It was darkish in hue - brown, he should say; the Russian woman was partial to that color. The thought came to him quickly; he stood bewildered. What if it were hers? Then how had it come here, on this narrow footpath, unless - Had the big car stopped at the top of the promontory and discharged its passengers there? But why should it have done so; for what possible reason?

He could think of none. Other women came this way - the path was not difficult. Other women wore brown veils. And yet that odd familiar fragrance - It seemed to belong to a foreign bizarre personality such as Sonia Turgeinov's.

Crushing in his palm the veil he thrust it into his pocket. He would find out more below, possibly; if she had actually passed this way. A feverish zest was born anew; the authorities were looking for her as well as for himself, he remembered. She, apparently, had so far cleverly evaded them; if he could but lead them to her he would not mind so much his own apprehension. Her presence in the locality at the same time the *Nevski* had been in the harbor would fairly prove the correctness of his theory of Miss Dalrymple's whereabouts. If he could now deliver the Russian woman into the hands of the law, he would have a wedge to force the powers that be to give credence to at least the material part of his story - that the prince had left port with the young girl - and to compel them to see the necessity of acting at once. That he, himself, would be held equally culpable with the woman was of no moment.

Fatigue seemed to fall from his shoulders. He went along more swiftly, inspired with new vague hopes. Down - down! The voice of the sea grew nearer; now he could hear the dull thud of the waves, then the weird whistling sounds that succeeded. Springing from a granite out-jutting to the sands, he looked eagerly, searchingly, this way and that. He saw no one. His gaze lowered and he walked from the dry to the wet strand. There he stopped, an exclamation escaping his lips.

A faint light, falling between black rocks, revealed fresh footprints on the surface of the sands, and, yes! - a long furrow - the marks of the keel of a boat. He studied the footprints closer, but without discovering signs of a woman's; only the indentations of heavy seamen's boots were in evidence. Mr. Heatherbloom experienced a keen disappointment; then felt abruptly reassured. The impress of her lighter tread had been eliminated by the men in lifting and pushing to launch the boat. Their boots had roughly kicked up the sand thereabouts.

He was fairly satisfied the woman had embarked. The seclusion of the spot favored the assumption; the fishing-boats were all either stranded, or at anchor, nearer the village. But why and whither had she gone? The ocean, in front, failed to answer the latter question, and his glance turned. On the one hand was the village; on the other, high, almost perpendicular rocks ran seaward, obscuring the view. It would not be easy to get around that point; without a boat it could not be done.

Mr. Heatherbloom began to walk briskly toward the village; the moon threw his shadow in odd bobbing motions here and there. Once he stopped abruptly; some one on the beach afar was approaching. A fisherman? Mr. Heatherbloom crouched back among the rocks, when the person came to a halt. Clinging to the shadows on the landward side of the beach the young man continued to advance, but cautiously, for a single voice might now start a general hue and cry. Beyond, closer to town, he could see other forms, small dark moving spots. Not far distant, however, lay the nearest boat; to get to her he had to expose himself to the pale glimmer. No alternative remained. He stepped quickly across the sand, reached the craft and strove to launch her. But she was clumsy and heavy, and resisted his efforts. The man, whoever he might be, was coming closer; he called out and Mr. Heatherbloom pushed and struggled more desperately - without avail! He cast a quick glance over his shoulder; the man was running toward him - his tones now rang out loudly, authoritatively. Mr. Heatherbloom did not obey that stern command to halt; instead he made a wild abrupt dash for the sea. The report of a revolver awoke the echoes and a bullet whizzed close. Recklessly he plunged into the water.

The man on the shore emptied his weapon, but with what success he could not tell. A head amid the dark waves was not easily discernible. Another and larger object, however, was plainly apparent about a hundred yards from land - a fishing-boat that swung at anchor. Would the other succeed in reaching it, for that was, no doubt, his purpose, or had one of the leaden missives told? The man, with weapon hot, waited. He scanned the water, then looked toward the town. A number of figures on the beach were hastening in his direction; from the pier afar, a naphtha put out; he could hear faintly the sound of the engine.

Suddenly, above the boat at anchor near the man on shore, a sail shot up, then fluttered and snapped in the wind. A moment later it was drawn in, the line holding the craft to the buoy slipped out, and the bow swung sharply around. Mr. Heatherbloom worked swiftly; one desire moved him - to get around that point before being overtaken - to discover what lay beyond. Then let happen what would! He reached for a line and hoisted a jib, though it was almost more canvas than his small craft could carry. She careened and plunged, throwing the spray high. He turned a quick glance back toward the naphtha. The sky had become overcast, and distant objects were not so easily discernible on the surface of the water, but he made out her lights - two! She was head on for him.

He looked steadily ahead again. The grim line of out-jutting rocks - a black shadow against the sky - exercised a weird fascination for him. He was well out in the open now where the wind blew a half-gale. His figure was wet from the sea but he felt no chill. Suddenly the hand gripping the tiller tightened, and his heart gave a great bound; then sank. Not far from that portentous point of land he saw another light - green! A boat was emerging from the big basin of water beyond. The starboard signal, set high above the waves, belonged to no small craft such as the woman had embarked in. The sight of it fitted a contingency that had flashed through his brain on the beach. The realization left him helpless now - his last opportunity was gone!

He shifted the tiller violently, recklessly. At that moment a shrill whistle from behind reminded him once more of the naphtha; he could have laughed. What was the wretched little puffing thing to him now? The single green light - that alone was the all in all. It belonged to the *Nevski* he was sure; for one reason or another she had but made pretense of going to sea, and, instead, had come here - to wait. The woman was on her now, and, also - The thought maddened him.

Again that piercing whistle! The naphtha was coming

up fast; amid the turmoil of his thoughts he realized this vaguely. He did not wish to find himself delivered unto them yet - not just yet! A wilder recklessness seized him. Clouds sped across the heavens like gripping furies' hands; the water ran level to his boat's gunwales but he refused to ease her. All the while he was drawing nearer the single green light - a mocking light, signal of a mocking chase that had led, and could lead, to nothing. Still he went on, tossed by the waves - sport of them. He had to play the play out. Oh, to see better, to visualize to the utmost the last scene of his poignant drama of failure!

In the naphtha some one's voice belched through a megaphone; he laughed outright now. Come and get him, if they wanted him! He would give them as merry a dash as possible. His boat raced madly through the water - nearer, yet nearer the green light. Now a large dark outline loomed before him; he would have to stop, to come about in a moment, or - A great wave struck him, half filling his boat, but he did not seem to notice.

A dazzling white glow suddenly surrounded him; from the naphtha a search-light had been flashed. It fell on him fully, sprinkled over on the wild hurtling waves beyond, and just touched the side of the outgoing vessel. Mr. Heatherbloom looked toward the vessel and his pupils dilated. The light leaped into the air with the motion of the naphtha, and, in an instant was gone, but the impress of a single detail remained on his retina - of a side ladder, lowered, no doubt, for the woman, and not yet hoisted into place on the big boat.

The wildness of the sea seemed to surge through Mr. Heatherbloom's veins; he did not come about; he did

FREDERIC STEWART ISHAM

not try to. Now it was too late! That ladder! - he would seize it as they swept by. Closer his boat ran; a swirl of water caught him, threw him from his course. He made a frantic effort to regain it but without avail. The big steel bow of the great boat struck and overwhelmed the little craft.

CHAPTER XIV

THE CRISIS

On the *Nevski*, the lookout forward walked slowly back and forth. Once or twice he shook his head. But a few moments before the yacht had run down a small boat, he had reported the matter, and - the *Nevski* had continued ahead, full speed. She had not even slackened long enough to make the usual futile pretense of extending assistance to the unfortunate occupant, or occupants. His excellency, Prince Boris, evidently did not wish, or had no time, to bother with blunderers; if they got in his way so much the worse for them. The lookout, pausing to stare once more ahead, suddenly started. Though apathetic, like most of the lower class of his countrymen, he uttered a faint guttural of surprise and peered over the bow. A voice had seemed to rise from the very seething depths of the sea. Naturally superstitious, he made the sign of the cross on his breast while tales of dead seamen who came back played through his dull fancy.

Once more he heard it - that voice that seemed to mingle with the wailing tones of the deep! The little swinging lantern beneath the bowsprit played on his bearded face as he bent farther forward, and, with growing wonder not unmixed with fear, now made out something dark clinging to one of the steel lines that

FREDERIC STEWART ISHAM

ran from the projecting timber to the ship. It took the lookout a few moments to realize that this dark object that had a voice - albeit a faint one - could not be other than a recent occupant of the small boat he had seen disappear. This person must have leaped upward at the critical moment, and caught one of the taut strands upon which he had somehow managed to hoist himself and to which he now clung desperately. It was a precarious position and one that the motion of the yacht made but briefly tenable.

Satisfied that the dark object was a reality and not an unwonted visitation, the lookout began deliberately to unloosen a gasket. Moments might be eternity to the man below, but Muscovite slowness is not to be hurried. The yacht's bow poised in mid air a breathless instant; chaos seemed leaping upward toward Mr. Heatherbloom, when something - a line - struck and rubbed against his cheek. He seized and trusted himself to it eagerly. The sailor was strong; he pulled in the rope. Mr. Heatherbloom came up, but his strength was almost gone. He would have let go when iron fingers closed on his wrists, and after that he remembered no more.

He awoke in a berth in a fo'castle, and it was daylight. Through a partly-opened hatch he could see the fine spray that came over the side of the yacht. Amid misty particles touched by the sun shone a tiny segment of rainbow. This Mr. Heatherbloom watched with a kind of childish interest; then stretched himself more luxuriously on the hard bunk. It was very fine having nothing more important and arduous to do than watching prismatic hues; his thoughts floated back to long forgotten wonder-days when he had possessed that master-marvel of toys, a kaleidoscope, and on occasion had importantly permitted the golden-haired child in the big house on the top of the hill to -

The dream was abruptly dispelled by some one laying a tarry hand on his shoulder. Mr. Heatherbloom raised himself. The person had a characteristic Russian face. For a moment the young man stared at the stolid features, then looked around him. He saw the customary furnishings of such a place; hammocks, bags and chests, several of the last marked with Russian characters. A trace of color sprang to Mr. Heatherbloom's face; he realized now what boat he was actually on, and what it all meant to him. He could hardly believe, however, and continued to regard the upside down odd lettering, when the sailor, who had so unceremoniously disturbed him, motioned him to get out. Mr. Heatherbloom obeyed; he felt very stiff and somewhat light-headed, but he steadied himself against the woodwork. The sailor drew a dipperful of hot tea from a samovar and thrust it into his hand. He drank with avidity; after which the sailor made him to understand he was to follow.

The young man hesitated - a new risk confronted him. To whom would he be taken? The prince? He had once been standing in the area way of the Van Rolsen house when the nobleman had approached. Had the distinguished visitor then been so absorbed in the sight of Miss Dalrymple coming down the steps that he had utterly failed to observe the humble caretaker of canines? Possibly - and again possibly not. In the former contingency he might yet have a brief breathing-spell to think - to plan for the future, unless - There was another to reckon with - the woman he had met in the park, whose automobile he had attempted to follow. She, too, was on the boat! He had been her dupe once. Was he now to become her victim?

The young man's jaw set. There was no holding back now, however; he had to go on - and he did, with seeming indifference and bold enough step. At the top of the ladder the sailor passed him on to some one else - an officer - who led him this way and that until they reached a secluded part of the deck, where, near the rail, stood a tall dark figure, glass in hand. Until the last moment Mr. Heatherbloom had hoped it might be only the captain he would be called on to encounter, and that that august person would summarily dispose of him, ordering him somewhere out of sight, below, to work his passage in the sailors' galley, perhaps. He would have welcomed the most ignominious service to have found now a respite - to be enabled to escape discovery a little longer. But the wished-for contingency had not arisen. He faced the inevitable.

"The man, your Excellency!"

His excellency looked. He had been scanning the horizon and his expression was both moody and preoccupied. Mr. Heatherbloom bent slightly forward; his lids fell to conceal a sudden glitter in his eyes; his hand touched something hard in his pocket. If his excellency recognized him - There was one way - a last mad desperate way to serve, to save her. It would be the end-all for him, but his life was a very small thing to give to her. He did not value it greatly - that physical self that had been such an ill servant. He gazed at the prince now with veiled expectancy, his attitude seemingly relaxed, innocent of strenuosity. Would the prince's gaze flare back with a spark of remembrance? If in that tense instant it had done so, then -

But his excellency regarded Mr. Heatherbloom blankly; his eyes were emotionless.

"You mean the fellow we ran down?" The prince spoke as if irritated by the intrusion.

"The same, Excellency!" The officer stepped back. Mr. Heatherbloom did not move.

"What did you get in our way for?" The prince's voice had a metallic ring; he towered, harshly arrogant, over his uninvited passenger. "Don't you know enough to get out of the way?"

"It appears not, sir." Heatherbloom wondered at the sound of his own voice. It seemed to come, small and quiet, from so far off. His excellency had not recognized him, but was he suspicious? Maybe not. No one would be fool enough to get deliberately in the way of the fast-steaming *Nevski*. Small craft were numerous in the bay and accidents to them would happen. There was nothing so out of the ordinary for a big boat to run down a tiny craft. It was somewhat uncommon for any one in the wee boat to save himself, truly, but even in this feature of the present case the prince experienced but a mild interest.

"Who are you?" he said. "A fisherman?"

"Not exactly," answered Mr. Heatherbloom, "though sometimes I crab. I was crabbing yesterday."

As he spoke his gaze swept beyond to not far-distant cabin doors and windows. He and the prince were standing on the starboard side of the boat; it was this side that had faced the island when the young man had

FREDERIC STEWART ISHAM

gazed down upon the yacht from the big sand-hill, and fancied he had seen -

"What am I going to do with you?" The prince seemed more out of temper now. "My crew are all Russians and I don't want any of your - " He stopped; shifting lights played ominously in his gaze; a few dissatisfied lines on his face deepened. "I didn't ask you to come aboard," he ended with an angry gesture.

"Sorry to intrude!" Mr. Heatherbloom spoke at random. "But I really couldn't help it, don't you know. No time to ask permission."

His excellency frowned. Did he suspect in these words an attempt at that insidious American humor he had often vainly endeavored to fathom? Mr. Heatherbloom gazed at him now with seemingly innocent but really very attentive eyes.

A superb specimen of over six feet of masculinity, the prince was picturesquely attired in Russian yachting-garb while a Cossack cap adorned a visage as bold and romantic as any young woman might wish to gaze upon. And gazing upon it himself - that rather stunning picture the prince presented on his own yacht - a sudden chill ran through Mr. Heatherbloom. This titled paragon refused by Miss Dalrymple? A feudal lord who made your dapper French counts and Hungarian barons appear but small fry indeed, by contrast! The light of the sea seemed suddenly to dazzle Mr. Heatherbloom. A wild thought surged through his brain. Betty Dalrymple, bewildering, confusing, made up of captivating inconsistencies, had sometimes been accused by people of a capacity for doing the wildest things. Had she for excitement - or any other reason - eloped with the prince? Were they, perhaps, married even now? He dismissed the thought quickly. All the circumstances pointed against this theory; his original one was - must be - correct.

"Well, now you are here, I suppose I've got to keep you." The prince had again spoken.

"I suppose so," said Mr. Heatherbloom absently. He was studying now the near-by cabin windows. One, with beautiful lace and glimpses of pink beyond, caught his glance.

"What can you do?" Sharply.

"Oh, a lot of things!" Had the curtain waved? His heart thumped hard - he scarcely saw the prince now.

"Not manage a sail-boat, I'm convinced." He forced himself to turn again, as through a mist was aware of his excellency's sneering countenance. "Judging from your recent performance!"

"That was hardly a fair test," Mr. Heatherbloom replied anyhow. His thoughts were keyed to a straining-point; his glance *would* swerve; he strove his best to control it. She was there - there - Shrouds and stays seemed to sing the words. He would have sworn he caught the flash of a white wrist.

"Why not?" Was the prince still examining, questioning him? Again a primal impulse was suppressed, though his muscles were like whipcords. He yet compelled himself to endure the ordeal. What was the query about? Ah, he remembered.

FREDERIC STEWART ISHAM

"Well, you see, I must have lost my head." It was not a bright answer but he did not care; it was the best that occurred.

The prince strode restlessly away a few paces, then returned. "Were you ever at sea before?"

"I once owned a y -" Mr. Heatherbloom paused - with an effort resumed his part and a smile somewhat strained: "I once went on a cruise on a gentleman's yacht." Some one *was* in the state-room; was overhearing. His head hummed; the refrain of the taut lines rang louder.

"What as? Cabin-boy, cook?"

"Why, you see -" The prince certainly did not see him - he was once more staring away, over the dark water - "I acted in a good many capacities. Kind of general utility, as it were. Doing this, that, and the other!"

"'The other', I should surmise." Contemptuously.

Mr. Heatherbloom moved; the curtain had moved again. "Where are you going?" he asked a little wildly. "You see I might have important business on shore." Foolish talk, - yet it fitted in as well as anything.

The prince, for his part, did not at first seem to catch the other's words; when he did he laughed loudly, sardonically. "That is good; excellent! *You* have 'important business'!"

"Yes; important," repeated Mr. Heatherbloom. "I -" He got no further. His eyes met another's at the window, rested a moment on a woman's face which then suddenly vanished. But not before he realized that she, too, had seen him - seen and recognized. He had caught in that fleeting instant, wonder, irony, incredulity - a growing understanding! Then he heard a soft laugh - a musical but devilish laugh - Sonia Turgeinov's!

CHAPTER XV

THE SWORD OF DAMOCLES

Mr. Heatherbloom stood as if stunned, his face very pale. For the instant all his suppressed emotion concentrated on this woman - his evil genius - who had betrayed him before and who would betray him again, now. He waited, breathing hard. Why did she not appear? Why did not the blow fall? He could not understand that interval - nothing happening. Was she but playing with him? The prince had abruptly turned; apparently he had not heard that very low laugh. Bored, no doubt, by the interview, he had started to walk away, almost at the same time Mr. Heatherbloom had caught sight of the face at the window. As in a dream Mr. Heatherbloom now heard his excellency's brusk voice addressing a command to the officer, listened to the latter a moment or two later, addressing him.

"Come along!" The officer's English was labored and guttural.

Mr. Heatherbloom's eyes swung swiftly from the near-by door through which he had momentarily expected the woman to emerge. Involuntarily he would have stepped after the vanishing figure of the prince - what to do, he knew not, when -

"*Non, non,*" said the officer, intervening. "Hees excellenz dislikes to be - importuned." The last word cost the speaker an effort; to the listener it was hardly intelligible, but the officer's manner indicated plainly his meaning. Mr. Heatherbloom managed to hold himself still; he seemed standing in the center of a vortex. The prince had by this time gone; the woman did not step forth. This lame and impotent conclusion was out of all proportion to the seemingly inevitable. He could scarcely realize it was he - actually he! - who, after another pause, followed the officer, with scant interest, hardly any at all, to some inferno where flames leaped and hissed.

He could not but be aware of them, although the voice telling him that he would remain here, make himself useful, and, incidentally, work his way among the stokers, sounded very far off. He could have exclaimed scoffingly after the disappearing officer, not anxious to linger any longer than necessary here. Work his way, indeed! How long would he be permitted to do so? When would he be again sent for, and dealt with - in what manner?

He shoveled coal feverishly though the irony of the task smote him, for in feeding the insatiable beds, he was with his own hand helping to furnish the energy that wafted her, he would have served, farther and farther from the home land. Every additional mile put between that shore and the boat, increased the prince's sense of power. He was working for his excellency and against her. In a revulsion of feeling he leaned on his shovel, whereupon a besooted giant of the lower regions tapped his shoulder. This person - foreman of the gang - pointed significantly to the inactive implement. His brow was low, brutish, and he had a fist like a hammer. Mr. Heatherbloom lifted the shovel and looked at the low brow but, fortunately, he did not act on the impulse. It was as if some detaining angel reached down into those realms of Pluto and, at the critical moment, laid a white hand where the big paw had touched him.

The young man resumed his toil. After all, what did it matter? - some one would shovel the stuff. That brief revolt had been spasmodic, sentimental. Here where the heat was almost intolerable and the red tongues sprang like forked daggers before dulled eyes, brutality and hatred alone seemed to reign. The prince might be the prodigal, free-handed gentleman to his officers; he was the slave-driver, by proxy, to his stokers. He who dominated in that place of torment had been an overseer from one of the villages the prince owned; these men were the descendants of serfs.

Once or twice Heatherbloom rather incoherently tried to engage one or two of them in conversation, to learn where the yacht was going - to Southern seas, across the Atlantic? - but they only stared at him as if he were some strange being quite beyond their ken. So he desisted; of course they could not understand him, and, of course, they knew nothing he wished to know. In this prison a sense of motion and direction was as naught.

Fortunately Mr. Heatherbloom's muscles were in good condition and there was not a superfluous ounce on him, but he needed all his energies to escape the fist and the boot that day, to keep pace with the others. The perspiration poured from his face in sooty rivulets; he knew if he gave way what kind of consideration to expect. He was being tested. The foreman's eyes, themselves, seemed full of sparks; there was something tentative, expectant in their curious gleam as they rested on him. Heatherbloom now could hardly keep to his feet; his own eyes burned. The flames danced as if with a living hatred of him; in a semi-stupor he almost forgot the sword, without, that swung over him, held but by a thread that might be cut any instant.

He could not have lasted many minutes more when relief came; sodden sullen men took the places. Heatherbloom staggered out with his own herd; he felt the need of food as well as rest. He groped his way somewhere - into a dark close place; he found black-looking bread - or, was it handed to him? He ate, threw himself down, thought of her! - then ceased to think at all. The sword, his companions or specters no longer existed for him.

It may be some spiritual part of him during that physical coma, drew from a supermundane source beatific drafts, for he awoke refreshed, his mind clear, even alert. He gazed around; he, alone, moved. His companions resembled so many bags of rags cast here and there; only the snores, now diminuendo, then crescendo, dispelled the illusion. A smoking lamp threw a paucity of light and a good deal of odor around them. Was it night? The shadows played hide-and-seek in corners; there was no sound of the sea.

Mr. Heatherbloom moved toward a door. His pulses seemed to throb in rhythm with the engines whose strong pulsations shook those limp unconscious forms. He opened the iron door and looked out. Only blackness, relieved by a low-power electric light, met his gaze. He crept from the place.

Why did not some one rise up to detain him? Surely he was watched. He experienced an uncanny sense of being allowed to proceed just so far, when invisible fingers would pounce upon him, to hurl him back. The soot still lay on his face; he had seen no bucket and water. At the mouth of a tunnel-like aperture, he hesitated, but still no one sprang in front, or glided up from behind to interfere with his progress. He went on; a perpendicular iron ladder enabled him to reach an open space on the deserted lower deck. Another ladder led to the upper deck. Could he mount it and still escape detection? And in that case - to what end?

A bell struck the hour. Nine o'clock! He counted the strokes. Much time had, indeed, passed since leaving port. The yacht, he judged, should be capable of sixteen knots. Where were they now? And where was she - in what part of the boat had they confined the young girl? Come what might, he would try to ascertain. Creeping softly up the second ladder, he peered around. Still he saw no one. It was a dark night; a shadow lay like a blanket on the sea. He felt for his revolver - they had not taken it from him - and started to make his way cautiously aft, when something he saw brought him to an abrupt halt.

A figure! - a woman's! - or a young girl's? - not far distant, looking over the side. The form was barely discernible; he could but make out the vague flutterings of a gown. Was it she whom he sought? How could he find out? He dared not speak. She moved, and he realized he could not let her go thus. It might be an opportunity - no doubt they would suffer the young girl the freedom of the deck. It would be along the line of a conciliatory policy on the prince's part to attempt to reassure her as much as possible after the indignities' she had suffered. The watcher's eyes strained. She was going. He half started forward - to risk all - to speak. His lips formed a name but did not breathe it, for at that moment the swaying of the boat had thrown a flicker of light on the face and Mr. Heatherbloom drew back, the edge of his ardor dulled.

The woman moved a few steps, this way and that; he heard the swish of her skirts. Now they almost touched him, standing motionless where the shadows were deepest, and at that near contact a blind anger swept over him, against her - who held him in her power to eliminate, when she would - When? What was her cue? But, of course, she must have spoken already - it was inconceivable otherwise. Then why had the prince not acted at once, summarily? His excellency was not one to hesitate about drastic measures. Mr. Heatherbloom could not solve the riddle at all. He could only crouch back farther now and wait.

Through the gloom he divined a new swiftness in her step, a certain sinuosity of movement that suddenly melted into immobility. A red spot had appeared close by, burned now on blackness; it was followed by another's footstep. A man, cigar in hand, joined her.

"Ah, Prince!" she said.

He muttered something Heatherbloom did not catch.

"What?" she exclaimed lightly. "No better humored?"

His answer was eloquent. A flicker of light he had moved toward revealed his face, gallant, romantic enough in its happier moments, but now distinctly unpleasant, with the stamp of ancestral Sybarites of the

Petersburg court shining through the cruelty and intolerance of semi-Tartar forbears.

The woman laughed. How the young man, listening, detested that musical gurgle! "Patience, your Highness!"

The red spark leaped in the air. "What have I been?"

"That depends on the standpoint - yours, or hers," she returned in the same tone.

"It is always the same. She is -" The spark described swift angry motions.

"What would you - at first?" she retorted laughingly. "After all that has taken place? *Mon Dieu*! You remember I advised you against this madness - I told you in the beginning it might not all be like Watteau's masterpiece - the divine embarkation!"

"Bah!" he returned, as resenting her attitude. "You were ready enough for your part."

She shrugged. "*Eh bien?* Our little Moscow theatrical company had come to grief. New York - cruel monster! - did not want us. *C'en est fait de nous!* Your Excellency met and recognized me as one you had once been presented to at a merry party at the Hermitage in our beloved city of churches. Would I play the *bon camarade* in a little affair of the heart, or should I say *une grande passion*? The honorarium offered was enormous for a poor ill-treated player whose very soul was ready to sing *De Profundis*. Did it tempt her - forlorn, downhearted -"

She paused. Close by, the spark brightened, dimmed - brightened, dimmed! Mr. Heatherbloom bent nearer. "At any rate, she was honest enough to attempt to dissuade you - in vain! And then" - her voice changed - "since you willed it so, she yielded. It sounded wild, impossible, the plan you broached. Perhaps because it did seem so impossible it won over poor Sonia Turgeinov - she who had thrown her cap over the windmills. There would be excitement, fascination in playing such a thrilling part in real life. Were you ever hungry, Prince?" She broke off. "What an absurd question! What is more to the point, tell me it was all well done - the device, or excuse, of substituting another motor-car for her own, the mad flight far into the night, down the coast where save for that mishap - But I met all difficulties, did I not? And, believe me, it was not easy - to keep your little American inamorata concealed until the *Nevski* could be repaired and meet us elsewhere than we had originally planned. *Dieu merci!* I exclaimed last night when the little spitfire was brought safely aboard." Mr. Heatherbloom breathed quickly. Betty Dalrymple, then, had been with the woman in the big automobile -

"Why don't you praise me?" the woman went on. "Tell me I well earned the *douceur*? Although" - her accents were faintly scoffing - "I never dreamed *you* would not afterward be able to -" Her words leaped into a new channel. "What can the child want? *Est-ce-qu'elle aime un autre*? That might explain -"

An expletive smacking more of Montmartre than of the Boulevard Capucines, fell from the nobleman's lips. He brushed the ash fiercely from his cigar. "It is not so - it won't explain anything," he returned violently. "Didn't I once have it from her own lips that, at least, she was not -" He stopped. "*Mon Dieu!* That contingency -"

Suddenly she again laughed. "Delicious!"

"What?"

"Nothing. My own thoughts. By the way, what has become of the man we picked up from the sail-boat?"

The prince made a gesture. "He's down below - among the stokers. Why do you ask?"

"It is natural, I suppose, to take a faint interest in a poor fisherman you've almost drowned."

"Not I!" Brutally.

"No?" A smile, enigmatical, played around her lips. "How droll!"

"Droll?"

"Heartless, then. But you great nobles are that, a little, eh, *mon ami*?"

He shrugged and returned quickly to that other more interesting subject.

"*Elle va m'epouser!*" he exclaimed violently. "I will stake my life on it. She will; she must!"

"Must!" The woman raised her hand. "You say that to an American girl?"

"We're not at the finis yet!" An ugly crispness was

manifest in his tones. "There are ports and priests a-plenty, and this voyage is apt to be a long one, unless she consents -"

"Charming man!" She spoke almost absently now.

"Haven't I anything to offer? *Diable*! One would think I was a beggar, not - am I ill-looking, repugnant? Your sex," with a suspicion of a sneer, "have not always found me so. I have given my heart before, you will say! But never as now! For she is a witch, like those that come out of the reeds on the Volga - to steal, alike, the souls of fisherman and prince." He paused; then went on moodily. "I suppose I should have gone - allowed myself to be dismissed as a boy from school. 'I have played with you; you have amused me; you no longer do so. Adieu!' So she would have said to me, if not in words, by implication. No, *merci*," he broke off angrily. "*Tant s'en faut*! I, too, shall have something to say - and soon - to-night -!"

He made a swift gesture, threw his cigar into the sea and walked off.

"How tiresome!" But the words fell from the woman's lips uneasily. She stretched her lithe form and looked up into the night. Then she, too, disappeared. Mr. Heatherbloom stood motionless. She knew who he was and yet she had not revealed his secret to the prince. Because she deemed him but a pawn, paltry, inconsequential? Because she wished to save the hot-headed nobleman from committing a deed of violence - a crime , even - if he should learn?

The reason mattered little. In Mr. Heatherbloom's mind

his excellency's last words - all they portended - excluded now consideration of all else. He gazed uncertainly in the direction the nobleman had gone; suddenly started to follow, stealthily, cautiously, when another person approached. Mr. Heatherbloom would have drawn back, but it was too late - he was seen. His absence from the stokers' quarters had been discovered; after searching for him below and not finding him, the giant foreman had come up here to look around. He was swinging his long arms and muttering angrily when he caught sight of his delinquent helper. The man uttered a low hoarse sound that augured ill for Mr. Heatherbloom. The latter knew what he had to expect - that no mercy would be shown him. He stepped swiftly backward, at the same time looking about for something with which to defend himself.

CHAPTER XVI

THE DESPOT

Prince Boris, upon leaving Sonia Turgeinov, ascended to the officers' deck. For some moments he paced the narrow confines between the life-boats, then stepped into the wheel-house.

"How is she headed?"

An officer standing near the man at the helm, answered in French.

"This should bring us to" - the nobleman mentioned a group of islands - "by to-morrow night?"

"Hardly, Excellency."

The prince stared moodily. "Have you sighted any other vessels?"

"One or two sailing-craft that have paid no attention to us. The only boat that seemed interested since we left port was the little naphtha."

The nobleman stood as if he had not heard this last remark. About to move away, he suddenly lifted his head and listened. "What was that?" he said sharply.

FREDERIC STEWART ISHAM

"What, your Highness?"

"I thought I heard a sound like a cry."

"I heard nothing, Excellency. No doubt it was but the wind - it is loud here."

"No doubt." A moment the nobleman continued to listen, then his attention relaxed.

"Shall I come to your excellency later for orders?" said the officer as the prince made as if to turn away.

"It will not be necessary. If I have any I can 'phone from the cabin - I do not wish to be disturbed," he added and left.

"His excellency seems in rather an odd mood to-night," the officer, gazing after, muttered. "Nothing would surprise me - even if he commanded us to head for the pole next. Eh, Fedor?" The man at the helm made answer, moving the spokes mechanically. Nor' west, or sou' east - it was all one to him.

Prince Boris walked back; before a little cabin that stood out like an afterthought, he again paused.

Click! click! The wireless! His excellency, stepping nearer, peered through a window in upon the operator, a slender young man - French. A message was being received. Who were they that thus dared span space to reach out toward him? *Ei! ei!* "The devil has long arms." He recalled this saying of the Siberian priests and the mad Cossack answer: "Therefore let us ride fast!" The swaying of the yacht was like the rhythmic motion of his Arab through the long grass beyond the

Dnieper, in that wild land where conventionality and laws were as naught.

He saw the operator now lean forward to write. The apparatus, which had become silent again, spoke; the words came now fast, then slow. Flame of flames! What an instrument that harnessed the sparks, chased destiny itself with them! They crackled like whips. The operator threw down his pen.

"Excellency!" He almost ran into the tall motionless figure. "Pardon! A message - they want to establish communication with the *Nevski* - to learn if we picked up a man from -"

"Have I not told you to receive all messages but to establish communication with no one? *Mon Dieu*! If I thought -"

"Your excellency, can depend upon me," Francois protested. "Did not my father serve your illustrious mother, the Princess Alix, all his life at her palace at Biarritz? Did not -"

The prince made a gesture. "I can depend upon you because it is to your advantage to serve me well," he said dryly. "Also, because if you didn't - " He left the sentence unfinished but Francois understood; in that part of the Czar's kingdom where the prince came from, life was held cheap. Besides, the lad had heard tales from his father - a garrulous Gascon - of his excellency's temper - those mad outbursts even when a child. There was a trace of the fierce, or half-insane temperament of the great Ivan in the uncontrollable Strogareff line, so the story went. Francois returned to his instrument; his excellency's look swept beyond. He heard now only the sound of the sea - restless, in unending tumult. The wind blew colder and he went below.

But not to rest! He was in no mood for that. What then? He hesitated, at war with himself. "Patience! patience!" What fool advice from Sonia Turgeinov! He helped himself liberally from a decanter on a Louis Quinze sideboard in the beautiful *salle a manger*. The soft lights revealed him, and him only, a solitary figure in that luxurious place - master of all he surveyed but not master of his own thoughts. He could order his men, but he could not order that invisible host. They made him their servant. He took a few steps back and forth; then suddenly encountered his own image reflected in a mirror.

"Boris, the superb"; "a tartar toreador of hearts"; "Prince of roubles and kopecs"! So they had jestingly called him in his own warm-cold capital of the north, or in that merry-holy city of four hundred churches. His glance now swept toward a distant door. "Faint heart ne'er won -"

Had he a faint heart? In the past - no! Why, then, now? The passionate lines of the poets sang in his ears - rhythms to the "little dove", the "peerless white flower"! He passed a big hand across his brow. His heart-beats were like the galloping hoofs of a horse, bearing him whither? Gold of her hair, violet of her eyes! Whither? The raving mad poets! Wine seemed running in his blood; he moved toward the distant door.

It was locked - of course! For the moment he had forgotten. Thrusting his hand into his pocket, he drew out a key and unsteadily fitted it. But before turning it he stood an instant listening. No sound! Should he wait until the morrow? Prudence dictated that course; precipitancy, however, drove him on. Now, as well as ever! Better have an understanding! She would have to accede to his plans, anyway - and the sooner, the better. He had burned his bridges; there was no drawing back now -

He turned slowly the knob, applied a sudden pressure to the door and entered.

A girl looked up and saw him. It was a superbly decorated salon he had invaded. Soft-hued rugs were on the floor and draperies of cloth of gold veiled the shadows. Betty Dalrymple had been standing at a window, gazing out at night - only night - or the white glimmer from an electric light that frosting the rail, made the dark darker. She appeared neither surprised nor perturbed at the appearance of the nobleman - doubtlessly she had been expecting that intrusion. He stopped short, his dark eyes gleaming. It was enough for the moment just to look at her. Place and circumstance seemed forgotten; the spirit of an old ancestor - one of the great khans - looked out in his gaze. Passion and anger alternated on his features; when she regarded him like that he longed to crush her to him; instead, now, he continued to stand motionless.

"Pardon me," he could say it with a faint smile. Then threw out a hand. "Ah, you are beautiful!" All that was oriental in him seemed to vibrate in the words.

Betty Dalrymple's answer was calculated to dispel illusion and glamour. "Don't you think we can dispense with superfluous words?" Her voice was as ice. "Under the circumstances," she added, full mistress of herself.

His glance wavered, again concentrated on her, slender, warm-hued as an houri in the ivory and gold palace of one of the old khans - but an houri with disconcerting straightness of gaze, and crisp matter-of-fact directness of utterance. "You are cruel; you have always been," he said. "I offer you all - everything - my life, and you -"

"More superfluous words," said Betty Dalrymple in the same tone, the flash of her eyes meeting the darkening gleam of his. "Put me ashore, and as soon as may be. This farce has gone far enough."

"Farce?" he repeated.

"You have only succeeded in making yourself absurd and in placing me in a ridiculous position. Put me ashore and -"

"Ask of me the possible - the humanly possible -" He moved slightly nearer; her figure swayed from him.

"You are mad - mad -"

"Granted!" he said. "A Russian in love is always a madman. But it was you who -"

"Don't!" she returned. "It is like a play -" The red lips curved.

He looked at them and breathed harder. Her words kindled anew the flame in his breast. "A play? That is what it has been for you. A mild comedy of flirtation!" The girl flushed hotly. " Deny it if you can - that you didn't flirt, as you Americans call it, outrageously."

An instant Betty Dalrymple bit her lip but she returned his gaze steadily enough. "The adjective is somewhat strong. Perhaps I might have done what you say, a little bit - for which," with an accent of self-scorn, "I am sorry, as I have already told you."

He brought together his hands. "Was it just a 'little bit' when at Homburg you danced with me nearly every time at the grand duchess' ball? *Sapristi*! I have not forgotten. Was it only a 'little bit' when you let me ride with you at Pau - those wild steeplechases! - or permitted me to follow you to Madrid, Nice, elsewhere? - wherever caprice took you?"

"I asked you not to -"

"But with a sparkle in your eyes - a challenge -"

"I knew you for a nobleman; I thought you a gentleman," said Betty Dalrymple spiritedly.

Prince Boris made a savage gesture. "You thought -" He broke off. "I will tell you what you thought: That after amusing yourself with me you could say, *'Va-t-en!'* with a wave of the hand. As if I were a clod like those we once had under us! American girls would make serfs of their admirers. Their men," contemptuously, "are fools where their women are concerned. You dismiss them; they walk away meekly. Another comes. *Voila!*" He snapped his fingers. "The game goes on."

A spark appeared in her eyes. "Don't you think you are slightly insulting?" she asked in a low tense tone.

"Is it not the truth? And more" - with a harsh laugh - "I am even told that in your wonderful country the rejected suitor - *mon Dieu!* - often acts as best man at the wedding - that the body-guard on the holy occasion may be composed of a sad but sentimental phalanx from the army of the refused. But with us Russians these matters are different. We can not thus lightly control affairs of the heart; they control us, and - those who flirt, as you call it, must pay. The code of our honor demands it -"

"Your honor?" It was Betty Dalrymple who laughed now.

"You find that - me - very diverting?" slowly. "But you will learn this is no jest."

She disdained to answer and started toward a side door.

"No," he said, stepping between her and the threshold.

"Be good enough!" Miss Dalrymple's voice sounded imperiously; her eyes flashed.

"One moment!" He was fast losing self-control. "You hold yourself from me - refuse to listen to me. Why? Do you know what I think?" Vehemently. The words of Sonia Turgeinov - "*Est ce qu'elle aime un autre?*" - flamed through his mind. "That there is some one else; that there always was. And that is the reason you were so gay - so very gay. You sought to forget -"

A change came over Betty Dalrymple's face; she seemed to grow whiter - to become like ice -

"You let me think there wasn't any one; but there was. That story of some one out west? - you laughed it away as idle gossip. And I believed you then - but not now. Who is he - this American?" With a half-sneer.

"There is no one! - there never has been!" said the girl with sudden passion, almost wildly. "I told you the truth."

"Ah," said Prince Boris. "You speak with feeling. When a woman denies in a voice like that -"

"Let me by!" The violet eyes were black now.

"Not yet!" He studied her - the cheeks aflame like roses. "He shall never have you, that some one - I will meet him and kill him first - I swear it -"

"Let me by!"

"*Carissima!* Your eyes are like stars - the stars that look down on one alone on the wild steppe. Your lips are red flowers - poppies to lure to destruction. They are cruel, but the more beautiful -"

He suddenly reached out, took her in his arms.

The cry on her lips was stifled as his sought and almost touched them. At the same moment the door of the cabin, by which the prince had entered, was abruptly thrown open.

FREDERIC STEWART ISHAM

CHAPTER XVII

THE PRINCE IS PUZZLED

His excellency turned. The intruder's eyes were bloodshot from the glare of the furnaces, his face black, unrecognizable, from the soot. "What the dev - " began the nobleman, as if doubting the evidence of his senses.

He must have relaxed his hold, for the girl tore herself loose. She did not pause, but running swiftly to the inner door she had just turned toward, she hastily closed and locked it behind her. As she disappeared Mr. Heatherbloom stopped an instant to gaze after her; but the prince, with sagging jaw and amazement in his eyes, continued to regard only him.

"Who the - " he began again furiously.

The intruder's reply was a silent one. His excellency would have stepped back but it was too late. Mr. Heatherbloom's fist struck him fairly on the forehead. Behind the blow was the full impetus of the lithe form fairly launched across the spacious cabin. The prince went down, striking hard.

But he was up in a moment and, mad with rage, made a rush. The other, quick, agile, evaded him. The prince's muscles had lost some of their hardness from high living and he was, moreover, unversed in the great Anglo-American pastime. He strove to seize his aggressor, to strangle him, but his fingers failed to grip what they sought. At the same time Mr. Heatherbloom's arms shot up, down and around, with marvelous precision, seeking and finding the vulnerable spots. The prince soon realized he was being badly punished and the knowledge did not serve to improve his temper. Had he only been able to get hold of his opponent he could have crushed him with his superior weight. A stationary table, however, in the center of the room assisted Mr. Heatherbloom in eluding the wild dashes, the while he continued to lunge and dodge in a most businesslike manner.

Panting, the prince had, at length, to pause. His face revealed several marks of the contest and the sight did not seem displeasing to Mr. Heatherbloom. A quiet smile strained his lips; a cold satisfaction shone in the bloodshot eyes.

"Come on," he said, stepping a little from the table.

The prince did not respond to the invitation. His dazed mind was working now. Through bruised lids he regarded the soot-masked intruder - a nihilist, no doubt! His excellency had had one or two experiences with members of secret societies in the past. There was a nest of them in New Jersey. Though how one of them could have managed to get aboard the *Nevski*, he had no time just then to figure out. The nobleman looked over his shoulder toward a press-button.

"Come on!" repeated Mr. Heatherbloom softly.

FREDERIC STEWART ISHAM

The nobleman sprang, instead, the other way, but he did not reach what he sought. Mr. Heatherbloom's arm described an arc; the application was made with expert skill and effectiveness. His excellency swayed, relaxed, and, this time, remained where he fell. Mr. Heatherbloom locked the door leading into the dining *salle* - the other, opening upon the deck, he had already tried and found fastened - and drew closer the draperies before the windows. Then returning to the prince, he prodded gently the prostrate figure.

"Get up!" His excellency moved, then staggered with difficulty to his feet and gazed around. "You'll be able to think all right in a moment," said Heatherbloom. "Sit down. Only," in crisp tones, "I wouldn't move from the chair if I were you. Because -" His excellency understood; something bright gleamed close.

"Are you going to murder me?" he breathed hoarsely. His excellency's cousin - a grand duke - had been assassinated in Russia.

"I wouldn't call it that." The prince made a movement. "Sit still." The cold object pressed against the nobleman's temples. "If ever a scoundrel deserved death, it is you."

Plain talk! The prince could scarcely believe he heard aright; yet the thrill of that icy touch on his forehead was real. His dark face showed growing pallor. One may be brave - heroic even, but one does not like to die like a dog, to be struck down by a miserable unclean terrorist - hardly, from his standpoint, a human being - unfortunately, however, something that must be dealt with - not at first, under these circumstances, with force - but afterward! Ah, then? The prince's eyes seemed to grow smaller, to gleam with Tartar cunning.

"What do you want?" he said.

"Several things." Mr. Heatherbloom's own eyes were keen as darts. "First, you will give orders that the *Nevski* is to change her course - to head for the nearest American port."

"Impossible!" the prince exclaimed violently.

"On the contrary, it is quite possible. We have the fuel, as I can testify."

His excellency's thoughts ran riot; it was difficult to collect them, with that aching head. The fellow must be crazy; people of his class usually are, more or less, though they generally displayed a certain method in their madness, while this one -

"I must remind your excellency that time is of every importance to me," murmured Mr. Heatherbloom. "Hence, you will do what I ask, *at once*, or -"

"Very well." His excellency spoke quickly - too quickly. "I'll give the order." And, rising, he started toward the door.

"Stop!"

The prince did. Venom and apprehension mingled in his look. Mr. Heatherbloom made a gesture. "You will give the order; but here - and as I direct." His voice was cold as the gleaming barrel. "That 'phone," indicating one on the wall, "connects with the bridge, of course. Don't deny. It will be useless."

His excellency didn't deny; he had a suspicion of what was coming.

"You will call up the officer in command on the bridge and give him the order to make at once for the nearest American port. You will ask him how far it is and how soon we can get there? Beyond that, you will say nothing, make no explanations, or utter a single superfluous word."

"Very well." The prince, seemingly acquiescent, but with a dangerous glitter in his eyes, moved toward the telephone.

"One moment!"

The nobleman stopped with his hand near a receiver. His fingers trembled.

"You will speak in French. A syllable of Russian, just one, and -" Mr. Heatherbloom's expression left no doubt as to his meaning.

"Dog!" His excellency's swollen face became the hue of paper. An instant he seemed about to spring - then managed to control himself. "But why should I not speak in Russian? My officers know no French."

"A lie! Nearly all Russian officers speak French. I happen to know yours do." A newspaper article had made the statement and he did not doubt it. "Anyhow, you give the order in French and we'll see what happens."

The blood surged in the nobleman's face. The fierce desire to avenge himself at once on this man who threw the lie at him - august, illustrious - mingled, however, with yet another feeling - one of bewilderment. The fellow had spoken these last words in French, and choice French at that. His accents had all the elegance of the Faubourg Saint Germain.

"Quick!" The decision in the intruder's manner was unmistakable. "I have wasted all the time I intend to. My finger trembles on the trigger."

The prince, perforce, *was* quick. The telephone of foreign design, had two receivers. His excellency took one. Mr. Heatherbloom reached for the other and held it to his ear with his left hand. His right, holding the weapon, was behind the prince, as the latter poignantly realized. Ill-suppressed rage made his excellency's tones now slightly wavering:

"Are you there, M. le Capitaine?"

"Steady!" Mr. Heatherbloom whispered warningly in his excellency's free ear, emphasizing the caution with a significant pressure from his right hand. At the same time he caught the answer from afar - a deferential voice:

"*Oui,* Excellence." There was, fortunately, on the wires a singing sound that would serve to drown evidences of emotion in the nobleman's tone. "Excellence wishes to speak with me?" went on the distant voice.

"I do." The prince breathed fast - paused. "You will change the boat's course, and - " He spoke with difficulty. A warmer breath fanned his cheek; he felt a sensation like ice on the back of his neck. "Make for the nearest American port. How far is it?" Mr.

Heatherbloom's prompting whisper was audible only to his excellency.

"Five hours," came over the wire.

Mr. Heatherbloom experienced a thrill of satisfaction. They were nearer the coast than he had supposed. He knew the yacht had been taking a southerly course; he had considered that when the bold idea came to act as he was doing. Possibly the prince had been driven out of the last port by the publicity attendant upon Mr. Heatherbloom's presence there, before certain needed repairs had been completed. These, Mr. Heatherbloom now surmised, it was his excellency's intention to have attended to in some island harbor before proceeding with a longer voyage.

Only five hours!

"Good-by!" now burst from the nobleman so violently that Mr. Heatherbloom's momentary exultation changed to a feeling of apprehension. But M. le Capitaine had evidently become accustomed to occasional explosive moments from his august patron. He concerned himself only with the command, not the manner in which it was given.

"Eh? *Mon Dieu*! Do I hear your excellency aright?" His accents expressed surprise, but not of an immoderate nature. He, no doubt, received many arbitrary and unexpected orders when his excellency went a-cruising.

"Repeat the order." Heatherbloom's whisper seemed fairly to sting the nobleman's disengaged ear.

The latter did repeat - savagely - jerkily, but the humming wires tempered the tones. M. le Capitaine understood fully; he said as much; his excellency should be obeyed - Mr. Heatherbloom pushed the nobleman's head abruptly aside, covering the mouthpiece with his hand. Perhaps he divined that irresistible malediction about to fall from his excellency's lips.

"Hang it up," he said.

The nobleman's breath was labored but he placed his receiver where it belonged; Mr. Heatherbloom did likewise. Both now stepped back. Upon the prince's brow stood drops of perspiration. The yacht had already slowed up and was turning. His excellency listened.

"May I ask how much longer you are desirous of my company here?"

"Oh, yes; you may ask."

The boat had begun to quiver again; she was going at full speed once more. Only now she headed directly for the land Mr. Heatherbloom wished to see. Five hours to an American port! Then? He glanced toward the door through which the girl had disappeared. Since that moment he had caught no sound from her. Had she heard, did she know anything of what was happening - that the yacht was now turned homeward? He dared not linger on the thought. The prince was watching him with eyes that seemed to dilate and contract. A moment's carelessness, the briefest cessation of watchfulness would be at once seized upon by his excellency, enabling him to shift the advantage. The

FREDERIC STEWART ISHAM

young man met that expectant gleam.

"Sorry to seem officious, but if your excellency will sit down once more? Not here - over there!" Indicating a stationary arm-chair before a desk in a recess of the room.

The prince obeyed; he had no alternative. The fellow must, of course, be a madman, the prince reiterated in his own mind unless -

"I told your excellency I had no wish for a long sea voyage." A mocking voice now made itself heard.

The nobleman started, and looked closer; a mist seemed to fall from before his gaze. He recognized the fellow now - the man they had run down. The shock of that terrible experience, the strain of the disaster, had turned the fellow's brain. That would explain everything - this extraordinary occurrence. There was nothing to do but to humor him for the moment, though it was awkward - devilish! - or might soon be! - if this game should be continued much longer.

Mr. Heatherbloom glided silently toward the hangings near the alcove. What now? - the prince asked with his eyes. Mr. Heatherbloom unloosened from a brass holder a silk cord as thick as his thumb.

"If your excellency will permit me -" He stepped to the prince's side.

That person regarded the cord, strong as hemp.

"What do you mean?" burst from him.

"It is quite apparent."

An oath escaped the prince's throat; regardless of consequences, he sprang to his feet. "Never!"

A desperate determination gleamed in his eyes. This crowning outrage! He, a nobleman! - to suffer himself to be bound ignominiously by some low *polisson* of a raffish mushroom country! It was inconceivable. "*Jamais!*" he repeated.

"Ah, well!" said Mr. Heatherbloom resignedly. "Nevertheless, I shall make the attempt to do what I propose, and if you resist -"

"You will assassinate me?" stammered the nobleman.

"We won't discuss how the law might characterize the act. Only," the words came quickly, "don't waste vain hopes that I won't assassinate you, if it is necessary. I never waste powder, either - can clip a coin every time. One of my few accomplishments." Enigmatically. "And" - as the prince hesitated one breathless second - "I can get you straight, first shot, sure!"

His excellency believed him. He had heard how in this bizarre America a single man sometimes "held up" an entire train out west and had his own sweet way with engineer, conductor and passengers. This madman, on the slightest provocation now, was evidently prepared to emulate that extraordinary and undesirable type. What might he not do, or attempt to do? The nobleman's figure relaxed slightly, his lips twitched. Then he sank back once more into the strong solid chair at the desk.

FREDERIC STEWART ISHAM

"Good," said Mr. Heatherbloom. A cold smile like a faint ripple on a mountain lake swept his lips. "Now we shall get on faster."

CHAPTER XVIII

THE COUP

Mr. Heatherbloom, with fingers deft as a sailor's, secured the prince. The single silken band did not suffice; other cords, diverted from the ornamental to a like practical purpose, were wound around and around his excellency's legs and arms, holding him so tightly to the chair he could scarcely move. Having completed this task, Mr. Heatherbloom next, with vandal hands, whipped from the wall a bit of priceless embroidery, threw it over the nobleman's head and, in spite of sundry frenzied objections, effectually gagged him. Then drawing the heavy curtains so that they almost concealed the bound figure in the dim recess, the young man stepped once more out into the salon.

How still it suddenly seemed! His glance swept toward the door through which the young girl had vanished. Why had he heard no sound from her? Why did she not appear now? She must have caught something of what had been going on. He went swiftly to the door.

"Miss Dalrymple!"

No answer. He rapped again - louder - then tried the door. It resisted; he shook it.

"Betty!" Yes; he called her that in the alarm and excitement of the moment. "It's - it's all right. Open the door."

Again that hush - nothing more. Mr. Heatherbloom pulled rather wildly at the lock of hair over his brow; then a sudden frenzy seemed to seize him. He launched himself forward and struck fairly with his shoulder - once - twice. The door, at length, yielded with a crash. He rushed in - fell to his knees.

"Betty! Oh, Betty!" For the moment he stared helplessly at the motionless form on the floor, then, lifting the girl in his arms, he laid her on a couch. One little white hand swung limp; he seized it with grimy fingers. It was oddly cold, and a shiver went over him. He felt for her pulse - her heart - at first caught no answering throb, for his own heart was beating so wildly. The world seemed to swim - then he straightened. The filmy dress, not so white now in spots, had fluttered beneath her throat. He gazed rapturously.

"It'll be all right," he said again. "Darling!"

He could say it now, when she couldn't hear. "Darling! Darling!" he repeated. It constituted his vocabulary of terms of endearment. He felt the need of no other. She lay like a lily. He saw nothing anomalous in certain stains of soot, even on the wonderful face where his had unconsciously touched it when he had raised her and strained her to him one mad instant in his arms. In fact, he did not see those stains; his eyes were closed to such details - and the crimson marks, too, on her gown! His knuckles were bleeding; he was unaware of it. He was not, outwardly, a very presentable adorer but he became suddenly a most daring one. His grimy hand touched the shining hair, half-unbound; he raised one of the marvelous tresses - his hungry lips swept it lightly - or did he but breathe a divine fragrance? By some inner process his spirit seemed to have come that instant very near to hers. He forgot where he was; time and space were annihilated.

He was brought abruptly back to the living present by a sudden knock at the door without, which he had locked after entering that way from the deck. Mr. Heatherbloom listened; the person, whoever he was, on receiving no response, soon went away. Had they discovered what had happened to the foreman of the stokers whom Heatherbloom had struck down with a heavy iron belaying-pin? The man had attacked him with murderous intent. In defending himself, Heatherbloom believed he had killed the fellow. The chance blow he had delivered with the formidable weapon had been one of desperation and despair. It had been more than a question of his life or the other's. Her fate had been involved in that critical moment. He had dragged the unconscious figure to the shadows behind a life-boat. They would not be likely to stumble across the incriminating evidence while it was dark. Nor was it likely that the foreman's absence below would cause the men to look for him. The overworked stokers would be but too pleased to escape, for a spell, their tyrannous master.

Mr. Heatherbloom, standing near the threshold of the dressing-room, glanced now toward the little French clock without. Over four hours yet to port! How slowly time went. He turned out all the lights, save one shaded lamp of low candle-power in the cabin; then he did the same in the room where the girl was. No one must peer in on him from unexpected places. He looked up, and saw that the skylights were covered with canvas. Mr. Heatherbloom remained in the salon; he needed to continue master of his thoughts. In the dressing-room he had just now forgotten himself. That would not do; he must concentrate all his faculties, every energy, to bringing this coup, born on the inspiration of the moment, to a successful conclusion. Desperate as his plan was, he believed now he would win out. By the vibrations he knew the boat was still steaming full speed on her new course. The conditions were all favorable. They would reach port before dawn; at break of day the health officers would come aboard. And after that -

The telephone suddenly rang. Should he answer that imperious summons? Perhaps the man who had just knocked at the door had been one of the officers, or the captain himself, come in person to speak with his excellency about the unexpected change in the boat's course, or some technical question or difficulty that might have arisen in consequence thereof.

He looked toward the recess; between the curtains he caught sight of the prince's eyes and in the dim light he fancied they shone with sudden hope - expectancy. The nobleman must have heard the crashing of the door to the dressing-room. What he had thought was of no moment. A viperish fervor replaced that other brief expression in his excellency's gaze.

Once more that metallic call - harsh, loud, as not to be denied! Mr. Heatherbloom made up his mind; perhaps all depended on his decision; he would answer. Stepping across the salon, he took down the receivers. The singing on the wires had been pronounced; he could imitate the prince's autocratic tones, and the person at the other end would not discover, in all likelihood, the deception.

"Well?" said Mr. Heatherbloom loudly, in French. "What do you want? Haven't I given orders not to be -"

His voice died away; he nearly dropped the receivers. A woman answered. Moreover, the wires did not seem to "sing" so much now. Sonia Turgeinov's tones were transmitted in all their intrinsic, flute-like lucidity.

"What has happened, your Excellency?" she asked anxiously.

"Happened?" the young man managed to say. "Nothing."

"Then why has the yacht's course been changed? I can tell by the stars from my cabin window that we are not headed at all in the same direction we were going -"

He tried to speak unconcernedly: "Just changed for a short time on account of some reefs and the currents! Go to sleep," he commanded, "and leave the problems of navigation to others."

"Sleep? *Mon Dieu*! If I only could -"

Mr. Heatherbloom dared talk no more, so rang off. The prince might have been capable of such bruskness. Sonia Turgeinov had not seemed to suspect anything wrong; she had merely been inquisitive, and had taken it for granted the nobleman was at the other end of the wire. Mr. Heatherbloom strode restlessly to and fro.

Seconds went by - minutes. He counted the tickings of the clock - suddenly wheeled sharply.

* * * * *

The young girl stood in the doorway - he had heard and now saw her. She came forward quickly, though uncertainly; in the dim light she looked like a shadow. He drew in his breath.

"Miss -" he began, then stopped.

Her gaze rested on him, almost indistinguishable on the other side of the salon.

"What does it mean? Who are you?" She spoke intrepidly enough but he saw her slender form sway.

Who was he? About to explain in a rush of words, Mr. Heatherbloom hesitated. To her he had been, of course, but a conspirator of the Russian woman in the affair. Miss Van Rolsen had deemed him culpable; the detective had been sure of it. Would Miss Dalrymple think more leniently of him than mere unprejudiced people, those who knew less of him than she? His very presence on the yacht, although somewhat inexplicably complicated in recent occurrences, was *per se* a primal damning circumstance. But she spared him the necessity of answering. She divined now from his blackened features what his position on the yacht must be. He was only a poor stoker, but -

"You are a brave fellow," cried Betty Dalrymple, "and I'll not forget it. You interfered - I remember -"

"A brave fellow ! " It was well he had not betrayed

himself. Let her think that of him, for the moment. A poignant mockery lent pain to the thrill of her words.

"You rushed in, struck him. What then?"

"He won't play the bully and scoundrel again for some time!" burst from Mr. Heatherbloom. His tones were impetuous; once more he seemed to see what he had seen during those last moments on the deck - when he had been unable to restrain himself longer - and had yielded to a single hot-blooded impulse. "The big brute!" he muttered.

She seemed to regard him in slight surprise. "Where is he? What has become of him?"

"He is safe -"

"You mean you conquered him, beat him - you?" Her voice thrilled.

"You bet I did," said Mr. Heatherbloom with the least evidence of incoherency. Her words had been verbal champagne to him. "I gave him the dandiest best licking -" He stopped. Perhaps he realized that his explanation was beginning to seem slightly tinged with too great evidence of personal satisfaction if not boastfulness. "You see I had a gun," he murmured rather apologetically.

"But," said the girl, coming nearer, "I don't understand."

He started to meet that advance, then backed away a little. "I've got him safe, where he can't move, or bother you any more." Mr. Heatherbloom glanced over his shoulder; but he did not tell her where he "had him". "And the yacht's going back to the nearest American port," he couldn't help adding, impetuously, to reassure her.

"Going back? Impossible!" Wonder, incredulity were in her voice.

"It's true as shooting, Bet -"

She was too bewildered to notice that slight slip of the tongue. "It's a fact, miss," he added more gruffly.

"But how?" Her tones betrayed reticence in crediting the miracle. Yet this blackened figure must have prevailed over the prince or the latter would not have so mysteriously disappeared. "How did it happen?"

"Well, you see I just happened around."

"You, a stoker?"

Stokers, he was reminded by her tone, did not usually "happen around" on decks of palatial private yachts. He must seek a different, more definite explanation. He thought he saw a way; he could let her know part of the truth. "The fact is, I was looking for this boat at the last port she stopped at. I had cause to think you would be on her. Couldn't stop the yacht from going to sea, for reasons too numerous to mention, so I just slipped out and came aboard in a kind of disguise -"

"A disguise? Then you are a detective?"

"I think I may truthfully say I am, but in a sort of private capacity. When a really important case occurs, it interests me. Now this was an important case, and - and it interested me." He hardly knew what he was saying, her eyes were so insistent. Betty Dalrymple had always had the most disconcerting eyes. "Because, you see, your - your aunt was so anxious - and" - with a flash of inspiration - "the reward was a big one."

"The reward? Of course." Her voice died away. "You hoped to get it. That is the reason -"

He let his silence answer in the affirmative; he felt relieved now. She had not recognized him - yet. In the recess behind the draperies the chair in which his excellency was bound, creaked. Was he struggling to release himself? Mr. Heatherbloom had faith in the knots and the silken cords. The girl turned her head.

"Don't you think it would be better" - he spoke quickly - "for you to return to your cabin? I'll let you know when I want you and -"

"But if I prefer to stay here? May I not turn on the lights?"

"Not for worlds!" Hastily. "It is necessary they should not see me. If they did -"

He was obliged to explain a little of the real situation to her; of the stratagem he had employed. This he did in few words. She listened eagerly. The mantle of the commonplace, which to her eyes had fallen a few moments before on his shoulders, became at least partly withdrawn. She divined the great hazard, the danger he had faced - was facing now. Detective or not, it had been daringly done. Her voice, with a warm thrill in it, said as much. Her eyes shone like stars. She

FREDERIC STEWART ISHAM

came of a live virile stock, from men and women who had done things themselves.

"If only I, too, had a weapon!" she said, leaning toward him. "In case they should discover -"

"No, no. It wouldn't do at all."

"Why not?" the warm lips breathed. "I can shoot. Some one once taught me -"

She stopped short. A chill seemed descending. "You were saying -" he prompted eagerly.

But she did not answer. The sweep of her hair made a shadowy veil around her; his mind harked swiftly back. She had always had wondrous hair. It had taken two big braids to hold it; most girls could get their hair in one braid. He had been very proud, for her, of those two braids - once - with their blue or pink ribbons that had popped below the edge of her skirts. He continued to see blue and pink ribbons now.

Both were for some time silent. At length she stirred - seated herself. Mr. Heatherbloom mechanically did likewise, but at a distance from her. He tried not to see her, to become mentally oblivious of her presence, to concentrate again solely on the matter in hand. A long, long interval passed. Chug! chug! the engines continued to grind. How far away they sounded. Another sound, too, at length broke the stillness - a stealthy footfall on the deck. It sent him at once softly to the window; he gazed out. She followed.

"Are - are we getting anywhere near port?"

He did not tell her that it was not port he was looking for so soon as he gazed out searchingly into the night.

"What is it?" She had drawn the curtain a little. Her shoulder touched him.

Suddenly his arm swept her back. " What do you mean" - he turned on her sternly - "by drawing that curtain?"

"Was any one there?"

"Any one -" he began almost fiercely; then paused. The figure he had seen in that flash looked like that of the foreman of the stokers. In that case, then, the fellow was not dead; he had recovered. Through a mistaken sense of mercy Mr. Heatherbloom had not slipped the seemingly lifeless body over the side. Now he, and she, too, were likely to pay dearly for that clemency. Bitterly he clenched his hands. Had the man caught a glimpse of him at the window? A flicker of electric light, without, shone on it.

The girl started again to speak. "Hush!" He drew her back yet farther. Above, some one had raised the corner of the canvas covering the skylight. It was too dark, however, for the person, whoever it might be, to discern very much below. Neither Mr. Heatherbloom nor his companion now moved. The tenseness and excitement of the moment held them. The girl breathed quickly; her hand was at his sleeve. Even in that moment of suspense and peril he was conscious of the nearness of her - the lithe young form so close!

The creaking of the chair in the recess was again heard. Had his excellency caught sight of the person above?

FREDERIC STEWART ISHAM

Was he endeavoring to attract attention? And could the observer at the skylight discern the nobleman? It seemed unlikely. The glass above did not appear to extend quite over the recess. Through a slight opening of the draperies Mr. Heatherbloom, however, could see his captive and noticed he seemed to be trying to tip back farther in his chair, to reach out behind with his bound hands - toward what? The young man abruptly realized, and half started to his feet - but not in time! The chair went over backward and came down with a crash, but not before his excellency's fingers had succeeded in touching an electric button near the desk. A flood of light filled the place.

It was answered by a shout - a signal for other voices. Fragments of glass fell around; a figure dropped into the salon; others followed. The door to the deck yielded to force from without. Mr. Heatherbloom, though surprised and outnumbered, struggled as best he might; his weapon rang out; then, as they pressed closer, he defended himself with the butt of his revolver and his fist.

There could be but one end to the unequal contest. The girl - a helpless spectator - realized that, though she could with difficulty perceive what took place, it was all so chaotic. She tried to draw nearer, but bearded faces intervened; rough hands thrust her back. She would have called out but the words would not come. It was like an evil dream. As through a mist she saw one among many who had entered from the deck - a giant in size. He carried an oaken bar in his hand and now stole sidewise with murderous intent toward the single figure striving so gallantly.

" No, no!" Betty Dalrymple's voice came back to her

suddenly; she exclaimed wildly, incoherently.

But the foreman of the stokers raised the bar, waited. He found his opportunity; his arm descended.

CHAPTER XIX

AND THEN -

Mr. Heatherbloom regained consciousness, or semi-consciousness, in an ill-smelling place. His first impulse was to raise his hands to his aching head, but he could not do this on account of two iron bands that held his wrists to a stanchion. His legs, too, he next became vaguely aware, were fastened by a similar contrivance to the deck. He closed his eyes, and leaned back; the throbbings seemed to beat on his brain like the angry surf, smiting harder and harder until nature at length came to his relief and oblivion once more claimed him.

How long it was before he again opened his eyes he could not tell. The shooting throes were still there but he could endure them now and even think in an incoherent fashion. He gazed around. The light grudgingly admitted by a small port-hole revealed a bare prison-like cell. Realization of what it all meant, his being there, swept over him, and, in a semi-delirious frenzy, he tugged at his fastenings. He did not succeed in releasing himself; he only increased the hurtling waves of pain in his head. What did she think of her valiant rescuer now, he who had raised her hopes so high but to dash them utterly?

Some one, some time later, brought him water and gave him bread, releasing his wrists while he ate and fastening them again when he had finished. The hours that seemed days passed. During that time he half thought he had another visitor but was not sure. The delirium had returned; he strove to think lucidly, but knew himself very light-headed. He imagined Sonia Turgeinov came to him, that she looked down on him.

"*Mon Dieu*! It is my canine keeper; the man with the dogs. What a lame and impotent conclusion for one so clever! I looked for something better from you, my intrepid friend, who dared to come aboard in that thrilling manner - who managed to follow me, through what arts, I do not know. How are the mighty fallen!"

Her tone was low, mocking. He disdained to reply.

"Really, I am disappointed, after my not having betrayed who you were to the prince."

"Why didn't you?" he said.

She laughed. "Perhaps because I am an artist, and it seemed inartistic to intervene - to interrupt the action at an inopportune moment - to stultify what promised to be an unusually involved complication. When first I saw and recognized you on the *Nevski*, it was like one of those divine surprises of the master dramatist, M. Sardou. Really, I was indebted for the thrill of it. Besides, had I spoken, the prince might have tossed you overboard; he is quite capable of doing so. That, too, would have been inartistic, would have turned a comedy of love into rank melodrama."

Rank nonsense! Of course such a conversation could

not be real. But he cried out in the dream: "What matter if his excellency had tossed me overboard? What good am I here?"

"To her, you mean?"

"To her, of course." Bitterly.

The vision's eyes were very bright; her plastic, rather mature form bent nearer. He felt a cool hand at the bandage, readjusting it about his head. That, naturally, could not be. She who had betrayed Betty Dalrymple to the prince would not be sedulous about Mr. Heatherbloom's injury.

"Foolish boy!" she breathed. Incongruous solicitude! "Who are you? No common dog-tender - of that I am sure. What have you been?"

"What -" Wildly.

"There! there!" said half-soothingly that immaterial, now maternal visitant. "Never mind."

"How is she? Where is she?" he demanded, incoherently.

"She is well, and is going to be, very soon now, the prince's bride."

"Never."

"Don't let his excellency hear you say so in that tone. He thinks you only a detective, not an ardent, though secret wooer yourself. The Strogareffs brook no rivals," she laughed, "and he is already like a madman.

I should tremble for your life if he dreamed -"

"Help me to help her -" he said. "It will be more than worth your while. You did this for -"

She shook her head. "I have descended very low, indeed, but not so low as that. Like the bravos of old" - was it she who spoke bitterly now? - "Sonia Turgeinov is, at least, true to him who has given her the little *douceur*. No, no; do not look to me, my young and Quixotic friend. You have only yourself to depend upon -"

"Myself!" He felt the sharp iron cut his flesh. That seemed indubitable - no mere fantasy of pain but pain itself.

"Let well enough alone," she advised. "The prince will probably put you ashore somewhere - I'll beg him to do that. He'll be better natured after - after the happy event," she laughed. "Perhaps, he'll even slip a little purse into your pocket though you did hurt a few of his men. Not that he cares much for them - mere serfs. You could find a little consolation, eh? With a bottle, perhaps. Besides, I have heard these island girls have bright eyes." He could not speak. "Are you adamant, save for one?" she mocked. "Content yourself with what must be. It is a good match for her. The little fool might scour the world for a better one. As for you - your crazy infatuation - what have you to offer? *Tres drole!* Do dog-tenders mate with such as she? No; destiny says to her, be a grand lady at the court of Petersburg. I am doing her a great favor. Many American families would pay me well, I tell you -"

She paused. "You will smile at it all, some day, my

FREDERIC STEWART ISHAM

friend. You played and lost. At least, it was daringly done. You deceived even me over the telephone. 'Go to sleep,' forsooth! You commanded in a right princely tone. And I obeyed."

An instant her hand lingered once more near the bandage. It was ridiculous, that tentative, almost sympathetic touch. Then, she - a figment of disordered imagination - receded; there was no doubt about his light-headedness now.

They sent again bread and water, and, after what seemed an intolerable interval, he found himself eating with zest; he was exceedingly hungry. He also began to feel mentally normal, although his thoughts were the reverse of agreeable. Days had, no doubt, gone by. He chafed at this enforced inaction, but sometimes through sheer weariness fell into a semblance of natural sleep despite the sitting posture he was obliged to maintain. On one such occasion he was abruptly awakened by a light thrown suddenly on his face. He would have started to his feet but the fetters restrained him.

It was night; a lantern, held by a hand that shook slightly, revealed a face he did not know. He felt assured, however, of his mental lucidity at the moment. The new-comer, though a stranger, was undoubtedly flesh and blood.

"What do you want?" said the prisoner.

"A word with you, Monsieur." The speaker had a smooth face and dark soulful eyes. His manner was both furtive and constrained. He looked around as if uncomfortable at finding himself in that place.

"Well, I guess you can have it. I can't get away," muttered the manacled man.

"Miss Dalrymple sent me."

Mr. Heatherbloom's interest was manifest; he strove to suppress outward signs of it. "What - what for?"

"She wanted to make sure you were not dead."

The prisoner did not answer; his emotion was too great at the moment to permit his doing so. She was in trouble, yet she considered the poor detective. That was like her - straight as a string - true blue -

The visitor started to go. "Hold on!" said Mr. Heatherbloom, whose ideas were surging fast. This youth had managed to come here at her instigation. Had she made a friend of him, an ally? He did not appear an heroic one, but he was, no doubt, the best that had offered. Betty Dalrymple was not one to sit idly; she would seek ways and means. She was clever, knew how to use those violet eyes. (Did not Mr. Heatherbloom himself remember?) Who was he - this nocturnal caller? Not an officer - he was too young. Cabin-boy, perhaps? More likely the operator. Mr. Heatherbloom had noticed that the yacht was provided with the wireless outfit.

"How long have I been here?" he now asked abruptly.

"It is three days since monsieur was knocked on the head."

Mr. Heatherbloom looked down. "Three days? Well, it cost me a fortune," he sighed, remembering the role of detective that had been thrust upon him. "I could have stood for the sore head."

The other had his foot at the threshold but he lingered. "How much of a fortune? What was the reward?" He strove to speak carelessly but there was a trace of eagerness in his tones.

"You mean what *is* it?" returned Mr. Heatherbloom, and named an amount large enough to make the soulful eyes open. "And to think," watchfully, "one little message to the shore might procure for the sender such a sum!"

"Monsieur!" Indignantly. "You think that I would -"

"Then you *are* the wireless operator?"

"I was." Francois spoke more calmly. "His excellency has had the apparatus destroyed. He will take no chances of other spies or detectives being aboard who might understand its use."

The prisoner hardly heard the last words; for the moment he was concerned only with his disappointment. A sudden hope had died almost as soon as it had been born. "Too bad!" he murmured. Then - "How did you get here?"

"The third officer has the keys and our cabins are adjoining. I seized an opportune moment, slipped in, and took a wax impression of what I wanted. Then with an old key and a file - Monsieur is a great detective, perhaps, but I, too," with Gaston boastfulness, "can aspire to a little cleverness."

"A great deal," said Mr. Heatherbloom, the while his brain worked rapidly. Betty Dalrymple must have paid the youth well for serving her thus far. Thrift, as well as sentiment, seemed to shine from Francois' eloquent dark eyes. Could he be induced to espouse her cause yet further?

"Monsieur must not think I would prove disloyal to his excellency, my employer," spoke up the youth as if reading what had been passing through the other's mind. "There could be no harm in a mere inquiry as to monsieur's state of health."

" None at all," assented the prisoner quickly. "Though" - a sudden inspiration came to Mr. Heatherbloom - "contingencies may arise when one can best serve those who employ him by secretly opposing them."

"I don't understand, Monsieur," said Francois cautiously.

"The prince is a madman. By incurring the enmity of his Imperial Master he would rush on to his own destruction. Suppose by this misalliance, the very map of Europe itself were destined to be changed?"

The words sounded portentous, and Francois stared. He had imagination. The beautiful American girl had told him that this man before him was a great and daring detective. He spoke now even as an emissary of the czar himself. The prince was a high lord, close to the throne. These were deep waters. The youth looked troubled; Mr. Heatherbloom allowed the thought he had inspired to sink in.

FREDERIC STEWART ISHAM

"What is our first port?" his voice, more authoritative, now demanded.

Francois mentioned an island.

"When do we get there?"

"We are near it to-night but on account of the rocks and reefs, I heard the captain say we would slow down, so as not to enter the harbor until daybreak."

Daybreak! And then? Mr. Heatherbloom closed his eyes; when he again opened them they revealed none of the poignant emotion that had swept over him. "What time is it now?"

"About ten."

"My jailer - the third officer, you say - visits this cell once every night. Do you know what time he comes?"

"I shouldn't be here, Monsieur, at this moment, if I didn't know that. He comes in an hour, after his watch is over, with the bread and water - monsieur's frugal fare. And now" - those apprehensions, momentarily dulled by wonderment seemed returning to Francois - "I will bid monsieur -"

"Stay! One moment!" Mr. Heatherbloom's accents were feverish, commanding. "You must - in the name of the czar! - for the prince's sake! - for hers - for - for the reward -"

"Monsieur!" Again that flicker of indignation.

Mr. Heatherbloom swept it aside. "She has asked you

to help her escape?" he demanded swiftly.

Francois did not exactly deny. There were no listeners here. "It would be impossible for her to escape," he answered rather sullenly.

"Then she did broach a plan - one you refused to accede to. What was it?"

"Mere madness!" Scoffingly. "Mademoiselle may be generous, and *mon Dieu!* very persuasive, but she doesn't get me to -"

"What *was* her proposal? Answer." Sternly. "You can't incriminate yourself here."

Francois knew that. The cell was remote. There could be no harm in letting the talk drift a little further. He replied, briefly outlining the plan.

"Excellent!" observed Mr. Heatherbloom.

"Mere madness!" reiterated Francois.

"Not at all. But if it were, some people would, under the circumstances," with subtle accent, "gladly undertake it - just as you will!" he added.

"Oh, will I?" Ironically.

"Yes, when you hear all I have to say. In the first place, I relinquish all claim to the reward. Sufficient for me -" And Mr. Heatherbloom mumbled something about the czar.

"Bah! That sounds very well, only there wouldn't be

any reward," retorted Francois. "The prince would only capture us again and then -" He shrugged. "I know his temper and have no desire for the longer voyage with old man Charon -"

"Wait!" More aggressively. "I have not done. No one will suspect that you have been here to-nigh't?" he asked.

"Does monsieur think I am a fool? No, no! And now my little errand for mademoiselle being finished -"

"You can do as Miss Dalrymple wishes, achieve an embarrassment of riches, and run no risk whatever yourself."

"Indeed?" Starting slightly.

"At least, no appreciable one." Mr. Heatherbloom explained his plan quickly. Francois listened, at first with open skepticism, then with growing interest.

"*Mon Dieu*! If it were possible!" he muttered. South-of-France imagination had again been appealed to. "But no -"

"Remember all the reward will be for you" - swiftly - "sufficient to buy vineyards and settle down for a life of peace and plenty -" Francois' eyes wavered; any Frenchman would have found the picture enticing. Already the beautiful American girl had, as Mr. Heatherbloom suspected, surreptitiously thrust several valuable jewels upon the youth as a reward for this preliminary service. Having experienced a foretaste of riches, Francois perhaps secretly longed for more of the glittering gems and for some of those American dollars which sounded five times as large in francs. Besides, this man, the great detective, or emissary, inspired confidence; his tones were vibrant, compelling.

"And for you, Monsieur? - the risk for you - " Francois faltered.

"Never mind about me. You consent?"

The other swallowed, muttered a monosyllable in a low tone.

"Then - " Heatherbloom murmured a few instructions. "Miss Dalrymple is not to know."

"I understand," said Francois quickly. And going out stealthily, he closed and locked the door behind him.

CHAPTER XX

INTO THE INFINITE

The midnight hour drew near, and, above deck, tranquillity reigned. It was, however, the comparative quiet that follows a storm. A threatening day had culminated in a fierce tropical downpour - a cloud-burst - when the very heavens had seemed to open. The *Nevski*, steaming forward at half speed, had come almost to a stop; struck by the masses of water, she had fairly staggered beneath the impact. Now she lay motionless, while every shroud and line dripped; the darkness had become inky. Only the light from cabin windows which lay on the wet deck like shafts of silver relieved that Cimmerian effect. The sea moaned from the lashing it had received - a faint undertone, however, that became suddenly drowned by loud and harsh clangor, the hammering on metal somewhere below. Possibly something had gone wrong with a hatch or iron compartment door inadvertently left open, or one of the ventilators may have got jammed and needed adjusting. The captain, as he hastened down a companionway, muttered angrily beneath his breath about water in the stoke room. The decks, in the vicinity of the cabins, seemed now deserted, when from the shadows, a figure that had merged in the general gloom, stepped out and passed swiftly through one of the trails of light. Gliding stealthily toward the stern, this person drew near the rail, and, peering cautiously over, looked down on one of the small boats swung out in readiness for the landing party at dawn.

"Mademoiselle," he breathed low.

"Is that you, Francois?" came up softly from the boat.

He murmured something. "Is all in readiness?"

"Quite! Make haste."

The person above, about to swing himself over the rail, paused; a cabin door, near by, had been thrown open and a stream of light shot near him. Some one came out; moreover, she - for the some one was a woman - did not close the door. The youth crouched back, trying to draw himself from sight but the woman saw him, and coming quickly forward spoke. She thought him, no doubt, one of the sailors. He did not answer, perhaps was too frightened to do so, and his silence caused her to draw nearer. More sharply she started to address him in her own native Russian but the words abruptly ceased; a sudden exclamation fell from her lips. He, as if made desperate by what the woman, now at the rail, saw or divined, seemed imbued with extraordinary strength. The success or failure of the enterprise hung on how he met this unexpected emergency. Heroic, if needs be, brutal measures were demanded. Her outcry was stifled but Sonia Turgeinov was strong and resisted like a tigress. Perhaps she thought he meant to kill her, and in an excess of fear she managed to call out once. Fortunately for the youth, the hammering below continued, but whether she had made herself heard or not was uncertain. Confronted by a dire possibility, he exerted himself to

FREDERIC STEWART ISHAM

the utmost to still that warning voice. In frenzied haste he seized the heavy scarf she had thrown around her shoulders upon leaving the cabin and wound it about her face and head. The sinuous body seemed to grow limp in his arms. His was not a pleasant task but a necessary one. This woman had delivered the girl to the prince in the first place; would now attempt to frustrate her escape. Any moment some one else might come on deck and discover them.

"Quick! Why don't you come?" Betty Dalrymple's anxious voice ascended from the darkness.

The youth knew well that no time must be lost, but what to do? He could not leave the woman. She might be only feigning unconsciousness. And anyway they would soon find her and learn the truth. That would mean their quick recapture. Already he thought he heard a footstep descending from the bridge - approaching - With extraordinary strength for one of Francois' slender build, he swung the figure of the woman over the side, dropped her into the boat and followed himself. A breathless moment of suspense ensued; he listened. The approaching footsteps came on; then paused, and turned the other way. The youth waited no longer. The little boat at the side was lowered softly; it touched the water and floated away from the *Nevski* like a leaf. Then the darkness swallowed it.

"How far are we from the yacht now, Francois?"

"Only a few miles, Mademoiselle."

"Do you think we'll be far enough away at daybreak so they can't see us?"

"Have no fear, Mademoiselle." The voice of Francois in the stern, thrilled. "There's a fair sailing wind."

"Isn't it strange" - Betty Dalrymple, speaking half to herself, regarded the motionless form in the bottom of the boat - "that she, of all persons, and I, should be thus thrust together, in such a tiny craft, on such an enormous sea?"

"I really couldn't help it, Mademoiselle" - apologetically - "bringing her with us. There was no alternative."

"Oh, I'm not criticizing you, who did so splendidly." The girl's eyes again fell. "She is unconscious a long time, Francois."

The youth's reply was lost amid the sound of the waters. Only the sea talked now, wildly, moodily; flying feathers of foam flecked the night. The boat took the waves laboriously and came down with shrill seething. She seemed ludicrously minute amid that vast unrest. The youth steered steadily; to Betty Dalrymple he seemed just going on anyhow, dashing toward a black blanket with nothing beyond. It was all very wonderful and awe-inspiring as well as somewhat fearsome. The waves had a cruel sound if one listened to them closely. A question floating in her mind found, after a long time, hesitating but audible expression:

"Do you think there's any doubt about our being able to make one of the islands, Francois?"

"None whatever!" came back the confident, almost eager reply. "Not the slightest doubt in the world, Mademoiselle. The islands are very near and we can't help seeing one of them at daybreak."

"Daybreak?" she said. "I wish it were here now."

Swish! swish! went the sea with more menacing sound. For the moment Francois steered wildly, and the boat careened; he brought her up sharply. The girl spoke no more. Perhaps the motion of the little craft gradually became more soothing as she accustomed herself to it, for, before long, her head drooped. It was dry in the bow; a blanket protected her from the wind, and, weary with the events of the last few days, she seemed to rest as securely on this wave-rocked couch as a child in its cradle. The youth, uncertain whether she slept or not, forbore to disturb her. Hours went by.

As the night wore on a few stars came out in a discouraged kind of way. Heretofore he had been steering by the wind; now, that scanty peripatetic band, adrift on celestial highways, assisted him in keeping his course. When one sleepy-eyed planet went in, another, not far away (from the human scope of survey) came out, and Francois, with the perspicacity of a follower of the sea, seemed to have learned how to gage direction by a visual game of hide-and-seek with the pin-points of infinitude. Between watching the stars, the sea and the sail, he found absorbing occupation for mind and muscle. Sometimes, in the water's depressions, a lull would catch them, then when the wind boomed again over the tops of the crests, slapping fiercely the canvas, a brief period of hazard had to be met. The boat, like a delicate live creature, needed a fine as well as a firm hand.

His faculties thus concentrated, Francois had remained oblivious to the dark form in the center of the boat, although long ago Sonia Turgeinov had first moved and looked up. If she made any sound, he whose glance passed steadily over her had not heard it. She raised herself slightly; sat a long time motionless, an arm thrown over a seat, her eyes alternating in direction, from the seas near the downward gunwale, to the almost indistinguishable figure of him in the stern, the while her fingers played with a scarf - the one that had been wound around her head. Once she leaned back, her cheek against the sharp thwart, her gaze heavenward. She remained thus a long while, with body motionless, though her fingers continued to toy with the bit of heavy silk, as if keeping pace with some mercurial rush of thoughts.

A wastrel, she had been in many strange places, but never before had she found herself in a situation so extraordinary. To her startled outlook, the boat might well have seemed a chip tossed on the mad foam of chaos. This figure, almost indistinguishable, yet so steadfastly present at the stern of the little craft, appeared grim and ghostlike. But that he was no ghost - His grip had been real; certainly that. He had been, too, perforce, a master of action. She leaned her head on her elbow. Strangely, she felt no resentment.

The tired stars, as by a community of interest and common understanding, slowly faded altogether. The woman bent her glance bow-ward. The day - what would it reveal? She understood a good deal, yet much still puzzled her. As through a dream, she had seemed to hear the name, "Francois" - to listen to a crystalline voice, fresh as the tinkling bells in some temple at the dawn. The darkness of the sky fused into a murky gray, and as that somber tone began, in turn, to be replaced by a lighter neutral tint, she made out dimly the figure of the girl. As by a species of fascination, she continued to look at her while the morn unfolded slowly. From behind a dark promontory of vapor, Aurora's warm hand now tossed out a few careless ribbons. They lightened the chilly-looking sea; they touched a golden tress - just one, that stole out from under the gray blanket. The girl's face could not be seen; the heavy covering concealed the lines of the lithe young form.

As she continued to sleep - undisturbed by the first manifestations of the dawn - the woman's glance swept backward to him at the helm. The shafts of light showed now his face, worn and set, yet strangely transfigured. He did not seem to notice her; beneath heavy lids his quick glances shot this way and that to where wisps of mist on the surface of the sea partly obscured the outlook. Sonia Turgeinov divined his purpose; he was looking for the *Nevski*. But although he continued to search in the direction of the yacht, he did not catch sight of her. Only the winding and twining diaphanous veils played where he feared she might have been visible. An expression of great satisfaction passed over his features.

Then he swayed from sheer weariness; he could have dropped gladly to the bottom of the boat. Brain as well as sinew has its limitations and the night had been long and trying. He had done work that called for tenseness and mental concentration every moment. He had outlasted divers and many periods when catastrophe might have overwhelmed them, and now that the blackness which had shrouded a thousand unseen risks and perils had been swept aside, an almost over-powering reaction claimed him. This natural lassitude became the more marked after he had scanned the horizon in vain for the prince's pleasure-yacht.

His task, however, was far from over, and he straightened. To Sonia Turgeinov, his gaze and his expression were almost somnambulistic. He continued steering, guiding their destinies as by force of habit. Luckily the breeze had waned and the boat danced more gaily than dangerously. It threw little rainbows of spray in the air; he blinked at them, his eyes half closed. In the bow the old dun-colored blanket stirred but he did not see it. A glorious sun swept up, and began to lap thirstily the wavering mists from the surface of the sea.

Sonia Turgeinov spoke now softly to the steersman. What she said he did not know; his lack-luster gaze met hers. All dislike and disapproval seemed to have vanished from it; he saw her only as one sees a face in a daguerreotype of long ago, or looks at features limned by a soulless etcher.

"Do you see it?" he asked.

"What?"

"Trees? Aren't those trees?"

"I see nothing."

"You do. You must. They are there." He spoke almost roughly, as if she irritated him.

"Oh , yes. I think I do see something," she said, and started. "Like a speck? - a film? - a bird's wing, perhaps?"

FREDERIC STEWART ISHAM

In the bow the blanket again stirred. Then, as from the dull chrysalis emerge brightness and beauty, so from those dun folds sprang into the morning light a red-lipped, lovely vision.

"Trees," repeated the steersman to Sonia Turgeinov. "I am positive -" he went on, but lost interest in his own words. Fatigue seemed to fall from him in an instant; he stared.

From beneath her golden hair Betty Dalrymple's eyes flashed full upon him.

"You!" she said.

Mr. Heatherbloom appeared to relapse; his expression - that smile - vague, indefinite - again partook of the somnambulistic.

CHAPTER XXI

AN ANOMALOUS SITUATION

The most unexpected and extraordinary thing in the world had happened, yet Betty Dalrymple asked no questions. Had she done so, it is probable that Mr. Heatherbloom would have been physically unequal to the labyrinthine explanation the occasion demanded. For a brief spell the girl had continued to regard him and she had seemed about to speak further. Then the blue light of her gaze had slowly turned and her lips remained mute. He was glad of this; of course he would later have to tell something, but sufficient unto that unlucky hour were the perplexities thereof. Sonia Turgeinov had been surprised, too, but it was Betty Dalrymple's surprise that had most awakened her wonder. "Why, didn't you know it was he?" the dark eyes seemed to say to the young girl. "Who else, on earth, did you think it was?" The mystery for her, as well as for Betty Dalrymple, deepened. Only for Mr. Heatherbloom there existed no mystery; it was all now clear as day. He had done what he had set out to do. She would soon be enabled to find her way back to civilization. His present concern lay with the occupation of the moment.

The tree *was* a tree; this was the most momentous immediate consideration; a few more miles had established that fact with positiveness. But distances on the water are long, and they three would have to journey together on the sea yet a while. He bethought him of his duties, as host; these - his two passengers-were in his care.

"You should find biscuits in a basket and water in a cask," he said, speaking to both of them, and, at the same time, to immeasurable distance. "If you don't mind looking - I can't very well."

At that, a nervous laugh welled from Sonia Turgeinov's throat; she had to give way. Possibly the absurd thought seized her that all the tragedies and comedies might be simmered down to one thing. Were there biscuits in the basket? But Betty Dalrymple did not laugh; her eyes were like stars on a wintry night; her face was white as paper. It was turned now from the steersman - ahead. She saw the blur before them become a definite line of green; later she made out details, the large heads of small trees. The former looked like big overflowing cabbages; the trunks, beneath, sprawled this way and that, as the vagaries of the wind had directed their growth. In front of them and the vernal strip, a white line slowly resolved itself into moving foam. She - they all could hear it now, faintly - they were very near; no thunderous anthem it pealed forth; its voice seethed in soft cadences.

Mr. Heatherbloom, with sheet taut, ran his craft toward the sands but the boat grounded some little distance from the shore. It was useless to attempt to go farther so he let his sail out, got up and stepped overboard. The water was rather more than knee deep; he tugged at the boat and attempted to draw her up farther without much success. She was too heavy, and desisting from his efforts, he approached Miss Dalrymple. The young girl shrank back slightly, but seeming not to notice that first instinctive movement, he reached over and lifted her out. It was done in a businesslike manner and with no more outward concern than a Kikuji porter might have displayed in meeting the exigencies of a like situation. The bubbles seethed around Mr. Heatherbloom's legs; unmindful of them or the shifting sands beneath foot, he strode straight as might be for the shore. His burden was not a heavy one but it seemed very still and unyielding. He released her at the earliest possible opportunity and in the same matter-of-fact way (still that of a human ferry on the banks of the turbulent Chania) he returned for his other passenger. Around Sonia Turgeinov's rich lips a mocking smile seemed to play; she arose at once.

"How charming! How very gallant!" she murmured. "First, you nearly strangle one, and then -"

Her soft arm stole about his neck, and her warm breath swept his cheek as, stony-faced, he trudged along. This time his burden was heavier, although there were men who would not have minded that under the circumstances. The dark eyes, full of sparkles and enigmas, turned upon his frosty ones. But she did not see very far into that so-called medium of the soul; she received only an impression one gets in looking at a wall.

He put her down - gently. Whereupon, her dark brows lifted ironically. He, gentle - to her? Did she dream? She felt again that fierce clasp of the night before, and mentally told herself she would like to label him an artistic study in contrasts. Really the adventure began to be "worth while"; she felt almost reconciled to it. He had carried her off as the rough, old-fashioned pirates bear away feminine prizes from a town they have looted. From dog-tender to bucaneer - he appealed to her imagination. She experienced a childlike desire to sit down where he had left her and play with the shells. But instead she looked toward Betty Dalrymple. That young girl, however, did not return her regard, though the golden head, a few moments before, had lifted once, with a swift, bird-like motion toward Sonia Turgeinov, en route beachward. Now the girl's features were steadfastly bent away; whatever gladness she may have felt in thus, after many vicissitudes, reaching land safely, she kept to herself.

Mr. Heatherbloom resumed the task of porter; his next burden - the water-cask - was the heaviest of all. He struggled with it and once nearly went down, so tired was he, but he got it ashore, and the basket of biscuits, too, and some other things. The boat, floating more lightly, he now pulled to the strand; then he took out the spar and the sail. This done, he gazed around; the place was deserted by man, though of birds and crabs and other crawling objects there were a-plenty. Mr. Heatherbloom stood with knitted brow; it was a time for contemplation, visual and mental. For the latter he did not feel very fit as he strove to think what was best to do next. The other two - he still forced himself to keep to the purely impersonal aspect of the case - were his charges. Being women, they were mutually and equally (the mockery of it!) dependent on him. He was responsible for their welfare and well-being. In the sail-boat he had been captain; ashore, he became commandant, an answerable factor. He began to plan.

What kind of place had they come to? - was it big or small? - inhabited, or deserted? All this would have to be ascertained, later. Meanwhile, temporary headquarters were needed; he would erect a tent. The spar and boom served for the ridge and front poles, the sail for the canvas covering, the sheet and halyards for the restraining lines. Sonia Turgeinov again watched him; her interest was now of that vague kind she had sometimes experienced when the manager appeared on a darkened stage, with a fresh crackling manuscript. Then she had lolled back and listened to the first reading. She would have lolled back now - for the air was soporific - but, instead, she started suddenly. The old wound on Mr. Heatherbloom's head, heretofore concealed by the cap Francois had procured for him, had reopened as he exerted himself; he raised his hand quickly and seemed a little at a loss. She stepped to him at once.

"The scarf, Monsieur?"

"Thank you." He took it absently.

"It serves divers purposes," she murmured. And Mr. Heatherbloom, remembering the more violent employment he had found for it the night before, flushed slightly.

She added delicate emphasis to her remark by assisting him. With her own fingers she tied a knot, and rather painstakingly spread out the ends. He endured grimly. Miss Dalrymple appeared not to have observed the episode but, of course, it had in reality been all quite fully revealed to her. It was in keeping with certain circumstances of the past that the Russian woman should not be unmindful of him, her confrere in the conspiracy. That much was patent; but other happenings were not so easily reconciled. What had taken place on the deck of the *Nevski* in those breathless last few moments as they were escaping, was in ill conformity with those amicable relations which should have existed between the two. This man's presence in the boat, in the place of Francois, could be explained by no logical process with the premises she had at her command.

The bandage possessed a subtly weird and bizarre interest for the young girl. He had been injured. How? For what reason? Betty Dalrymple's mind swept, seemingly without very definite cause, to another scene, one of violence. Again she heard the crashing of glass and saw forms leaping into the cabin. Her thoughts reverted, on the instant, to the unknown helper she had been obliged to leave behind. Somehow, real as he had been, he seemed at this moment strangely apart, something in the abstract. Then all illusive speculations merged abruptly into a realization that needed no demonstration. Sonia Turgeinov possessed a certain outre attractiveness the young girl had never noted before. The violet eyes, shining through the long shading lashes, rested a moment on her; then passed steadily beyond.

"I'm off for a look around." Mr. Heatherbloom, having transferred their meager possessions to the tent, now addressed Miss Dalrymple, or Sonia Turgeinov, or an indefinite space between them. "Better stay right here while I'm gone." His tones had a firm accent. "Sorry there are only biscuits for breakfast, but perhaps there'll be better fare before long. If you should move around" - his eye lingered authoritatively on Betty Dalrymple - "keep to the beach."

"How very solicitous!" laughed Sonia Turgeinov as the young man strode off. "That was intended especially

for you, Mademoiselle. As for me, it does not matter."
With a shrug. "I might stroll into the wood, be
devoured by wild beasts, and who would care?"

Betty Dalrymple did not answer.

"A truce, Mademoiselle!" said the other in the same
gay tone. "I know very well what you think of me. You
told me very clearly on the *Nevski*, and before that, on
shore. In this instance, however, since it is through no
fault or choice of mine that we are thrown thus closely
together, would it not be well to make the best of the
situation?"

"There seems, indeed, no choice in the matter,"
answered the young girl coldly.

"None, unless like those in the admirable play, we
elect to pitch our respective camps at different parts of
the beach. But that would be absurd, wouldn't it?
Besides, I have my punishment - no light one for Sonia
Turgeinov who herself has been accustomed to a little
adulation in the past. I am *de trop*."

"*De trop*?" There was a faint uplifting of the brow.
"*You* should not be altogether that."

"You mean I should be very friendly with him, my
colleague and confidant, *n'est ce pas*?" Sonia's dark
eyes swept swiftly the proud lovely face. "In truth he
proved an able assistant." Her voice was a little
mocking. "What if I should tell you it was he who
planned it all - devised the ways and means?" A statue
could, not have been more immovable than Betty
Dalrymple. "Or," suddenly, "what if I should say quite
- *au contraire*." The girl stirred. Sonia Turgeinov

seemed to ruminate. "Should I be so forgiving - after last night?" she murmured. "It would be inconsistent, wouldn't it? - or angelic? And I am no angel."

The girl's lips started to form a question but she did not speak. Afar, Mr. Heatherbloom's figure could be seen, almost at the vanishing point. He was toiling up an incline. Then the green foliage swallowed him. Sonia Turgeinov smiled at vacancy. "Though I do owe him a little," she went on, half meditative. "He *was* kind to me in the park. He was sorry for me. Think of it, and without admiring me. Other men have professed for poor Sonia Turgeinov a little interest or solicitude at divers times and places, but it has always been accompanied with something else. Is that beyond the understanding of your pure soul, nourished in a hothouse, Mademoiselle?" There was a sudden hard ring of rebellion in her tones. "Am I handsome? Your eyes said it not long ago. *Ma foi*!" Her voice becoming light again. "It was Parsifal himself who talked with me in the park - that place for rendezvous and romances." Her thoughts leaped over time and space. "The first light of the sun revealed to you this day the last face you expected to see. It was as if a bit of miracle, or a little diablerie had happened. I, too, was in a haze, not so great - though on the deck the night before I little expected to encounter one I had last seen in chains, a prisoner -"

"A prisoner - in chains - he -" Betty Dalrymple stared.

"You did not know? What on earth did you expect? That the prince would give him the *suite de luxe* after the beating his excellency received -"

"The beating?" half-stammered the girl. "Then the man

in the salon who claimed to be a detective was -"

"What? He claimed that?" laughed Sonia Turgeinov. *"Tres drole!"*

But Betty Dalrymple did not laugh. Her eyes, bent seaward, saw nothing now of the leaping waves; her face was fixed as a cameo's. Only her hair stirred, wind-tossed, all in motion like her thoughts. And regarding her, Sonia Turgeinov's eyes began to harden a little. Did the woman regret for the moment what she had said, divining again some play within a play? Yet what could there be in common between this beautiful heiress and the *gardeurde chiens*? No! it was absurd to conceive anything of the kind. Nevertheless Sonia Turgeinov unaccountably began to experience a vague hostility for the young girl; this she might partly attribute to the great gaps of convention separating them. Her own life, in confused pictures, surged panorama-like before her mental vision: The garret beginning; the cold and hunger hardships; the beatings, when a child; the girl problems - so hard; the woman's - Faugh! what a life! Would that the flame of the artist had burned more brightly or not at all. She tried to imagine what she would have been, if she, too, had been born to a golden cradle.

A great ennui swept over her. How old she felt on a sudden! And how homesick, too. Yes; that was it - homesickness. She could have stretched out her arms toward her much beloved and, sometimes, a little hated, Russia. The bright domes of her native city seemed to shine now in her eyes. She walked in spirit the stony pavement of the Kremlin. Cruelty, intolerance, suffering - all these reigned in the city of extremes, but she would have kissed even the cold marble at the feet of dead tyrants, the way the people did, if she could have stood at that moment in one of the old, old sacred places. Her brief flight into the new world had led her to no pots of gold at rainbow end. The little honorarium from his excellency for her part in this adventure, she did not want now. She regretted that she had ever embarked upon it. What penalty might she not have to pay yet? The law, with dragon fingers would reach out - no doubt was reaching out now - to grip her. Well, let it.

A crisp, matter-of-fact voice - concealing any agitation the speaker may have felt - broke in upon these varied reflections. Mr. Heatherbloom, rather out of breath but quiet and determined, stood before them.

"Miss Dalrymple! - Mademoiselle! There is no occasion for alarm but it will be necessary; for us to leave here at once!"

CHAPTER XXII

AN UNEXPECTED OFFER

"To leave?" It was Sonia Turgeinov who spoke. "You mean -" Her eyes turned oceanward but saw nothing.

He made a quick gesture toward a break in the outline of the shore where the island swept around. "Beyond!" he said succinctly and she had no doubt as to his meaning. The tent he had put up where it could not be seen from the sea. But their boat - He looked at the little craft, a too distinct object on the sands. Those on a vessel skirting the shore could not fail to discover that incriminating bit of evidence with their glasses. And there was no way of getting rid of it. He could not destroy it with his bare hands. It was unsinkable. If he set it adrift, wind and sea would drive it straight back.

"They probably discovered our absence about day-break and surmised correctly the direction the breeze would carry us," he muttered half bitterly. "We must go at once." These last words he spoke firmly.

"But where?" Again it was Sonia Turgeinov who questioned him. Betty Dalrymple remained silent; her eyes shone with a new inscrutable light; her cheek, though pale, had the warmth of a live pearl. She touched the sands with the tip of her shoe.

FREDERIC STEWART ISHAM

But he did not regard her, nor did he answer Sonia Turgeinov. Going to the tent, he bent over the basket of biscuits and hastily filled his pockets. Then, throwing a woman's heavy cloak over his arm, he stepped quickly to Miss Dalrymple's side.

"Come," he said laconically.

Her foot, Cinderella's for daintiness, ceased its motion; she turned at once. Around her lips a strange little smile flitted but faded almost immediately. Save for her straightness and that proud characteristic poise of the head, she might have seemed, at that moment of emergency, a veritable Griselda for acquiescence. He started to walk away, when -

"What about me?" cried Sonia Turgeinov.

"You can come or you can stay," said Mr. Heather-bloom. "The chances are that the prince will see the boat, land and get you."

"And if he doesn't?"

"There are plenty of biscuits, and I'll send back for you when I can."

"That prospect is not very inviting," she demurred. "Suppose I elect not to risk it - to go with you?"

"It is for you to decide, and quickly," he said in a cold crisp tone.

"You dismiss my fate bruskly, Monsieur," she returned.

"There is no time to bandy words, Madam," he retorted warmly. "I am not oblivious to you - I trust I would not be to any woman - but every minute now is precious."

"Of course!" An instant she looked at the girl and a spark appeared in the dark eyes. Then Sonia Turgeinov's features abruptly relaxed and she waved her hand carelessly. "I have decided," she said in her old manner. "Go! My best adieus, Monsieur - Mademoiselle." With a gay courtesy. "Farewell! babes in the wood!" Her voice was once more mocking. They moved silently away but before they had gone far enough to disappear in the forest she suddenly ran toward them. "No, no!" she said in a different voice. "I have changed my mind. It is such a tiny, thing, that boat - in the glare and shine. They might not see it, and then -" She shuddered, "How frightfully lonesome! - the terrible nights -"

He made an impatient gesture. "After me, then! You, Miss Dalrymple, will come last."

"Ah, you think I am coming because I may wish to help them?" Sonia Turgeinov said quickly.

"I intend to take no chances," he returned in the same tone. And the three moved on.

He set a sharp pace; if there was need for haste at all it was now, at the beginning of their flight. They plunged deeper into the forest; no one spoke; only the crackling under foot and certain wood sounds broke the stillness. Unfortunately the soil was soft so that their footprints might be followed by any one versed in woodcraft. At times they were forced to skirt unusually thick places, but in spite of these deviations Mr. Heatherbloom was enabled generally to keep to their course by consulting a small compass he had found in the boat. It was essential to maintain as straight a line as possible. People sometimes walked round and round in forests; he took no chance of that; better a moment lost now and then, while stopping to wait for the quivering pointer to settle, than returning, perhaps, to the very spot they had left.

As thus they advanced, often he looked around to reassure himself that the young girl, in spite of the roughness of the way, yet followed. Once Sonia Turgeinov arrested that swift backward look; her own shone with curiosity.

"How in heaven's name did you do it, Monsieur?" she asked suddenly, drawing nearer. "Get out of that cell, I mean. When last I saw you on the ship, you were as securely fastened as a prisoner in the fortress at Petersburg. Of course you must have had some one to help -"

He answered coldly, recalling a promise to protect Francois. He could, however, and did, tell her the truth in this without involving the youth. "When the third officer, my jailer, came to the cell and released my hands - well, I did the best I could, surprised him, got the keys and left him there in my stead. A little Jap trick for handling men that I learned in San Francisco long ago," he added.

Her dark eyes lingered on him not without a trace of admiration. "Mademoiselle is fortunate, indeed, in her champion," she murmured. "And yet that does not explain the preparations for departure - the provisions in the boat - other little details. How came you by that compass, for example?"

"It explains all that will be explained."

"Which means, once more, you do not trust me?" She shrugged. "*Eh bien!*" And again they went on in silence.

Toward noon, reaching a fringe of the forest, they found before them a wide open space where the ground was higher and dry, but the walking more difficult. The grass, long and tenacious, twined snake-like around their ankles; they had to go more slowly, but reached, at length, the top of the eminence. Here Mr. Heatherbloom stopped. They ate their biscuit and rested, but only for a brief while. Scanning the distance, in the direction they had come, he suddenly discerned moving forms on the farthest edge of the open space - forms which advanced toward them. No doubt as to their purpose could be entertained; his excellency had landed and was already in pursuit. A smoldering fire leaped from Mr. Heatherbloom's eyes while rage that she should thus be driven harder filled his breast. Fool! that he had not killed the prince when opportunity had offered that night in the cabin. His clemency might - probably would - cost her dear.

"We've got to go on, and faster," said the young man. His hands were clenched; his arms were stiff at his side. "Can you do it?" he asked Betty Dalrymple. She answered; standing in a green recess, she had never appeared more beautiful to him than in that moment of peril. Green and red things flashed behind her - tiny feathered creatures that shone like jewels. The dewdrops from the branches in sunless places were glistening brilliants in the gold of her hair. But he had no time to gaze. The figures were drawing nearer.

"You used to be able to run, Betty. It seems as if it's all my fault" - hoarsely - "but you'll have to do so now."

Again that ready response from her! Did she, in the excitement of the moment, call him by a Christian name not Horatio? He did not take cognizance of it; neither did Sonia Turgeinov seem to.

The latter spoke quickly: "I remain here."

"Of course," said Mr. Heatherbloom, with a glance back toward the open space.

She overlooked the significance or bitterness in his accent. "Keep to the right," she said swiftly. "Believe me or not, I'll send them to the left. It's your only chance. Otherwise they would overtake you in an hour. Among the prince's men are Cossacks trained to feats of endurance."

"You would do that?" He looked at her quickly. The dark eyes did not swerve from the gray ones.

"Did I betray you on the boat?" said Sonia Turgeinov rather haughtily.

"No," he conceded.

"And yet I knew you! You know that," she affirmed.

"Yes; you knew me." Slowly.

"Did I tell his excellency who you were, when he had you, a prisoner?" she demanded.

And - "No," he was obliged to say again.

"See." She took from her breast a tiny cross. "I had that as a child. Would I kiss it, and - tell you a lie in the next breath?" He did not answer. "I have lived up to the letter of my contract with his excellency. It is at an end. Perhaps I am a little sorry for my own part" - with a laugh slightly reckless - "or maybe" - with a flash of seriousness - "I have become, in the least, afraid. Your laws are very severe, and - I had not counted on mademoiselle's steadfast resistance to - *mon Dieu!* - a prince who had been considered irresistible - whose principality is larger than one of your states - who would have made her, in truth, a czaritza. I had fancied," in a rush of words, "the mad episode might end as it did in the prince's favorite *Fire and Sword* trilogy, with wedding-bells and rejoicing." She paused abruptly. "I had also not counted on the all-important possibility that mademoiselle might have bestowed her heart on another -"

"Madam!" It was Betty Dalrymple who spoke quickly.

Sonia Turgeinov laughed maliciously. "Go," she said, "or" - almost fiercely - "I may change my mind."

They went; Sonia Turgeinov turned and looked out over the open space. The approaching figures were now much nearer.

CHAPTER XXIII

STARLIGHT

Dusk had begun to fall, but still two figures went on through the forest - slowly, with obvious effort. One turned often to the other, held back a branch, or proffered such service as he might over rough places, for Betty Dalrymple's movements were no longer those of a lithe wood-nymph; she had never felt so weary before. The first shades of twilight made it harder to distinguish their way amid intervening objects, and once an elastic bit of underbrush struck her sharply in the face. The blow smarted like the touch of a whip but she only smiled faintly. The momentary sting spurred her on faster, until her foot caught and she stumbled and would have fallen except that Mr. Heatherbloom had turned at that moment and put out an arm.

"Forgive me." His voice was full of contrition. "It has been brutal to make you go on like this, but I had to."

"It doesn't matter." The slender form slid from him over-quickly. "You, too, must be very tired," she said with breath coming fast.

He glanced swiftly back; listened. "We'll rest here," he commanded. "We've got to. I should have stopped before , but" - the words came in a harsher staccato - "I dared not."

"I'll be all right in a few moments," she answered, resting on a fallen log, "and then -"

"No, no," he said in a tone of finality. "After all, there is small likelihood they'll find us now. Besides, it will soon be too dark to go on. Fortunately, the night is warm, and I've got this cloak for you."

"And for yourself?" Her voice was very low and quiet, or perhaps it seemed so because here, in the little recess in the great wood, the hush was most pronounced.

"Me?" he laughed. "You seem to forget I'm one of the happy brotherhood that just drop down anywhere. Shouldn't know what to do with a silk eiderdown if I had one."

His gaiety sounded rather forced. She was silent and the quietude seemed oppressive. The girl leaned back to a great tree trunk and looked up. The sky wore an ocher hue against which the branches quivered in zigzags of blackness. Mr. Heatherbloom moved apart to watch, but still he neither saw nor heard sign of any one drawing near. The sad ocher merged into a somber blue; the stars came out, one by one, then in shoals. She could hardly see him now, so fast had the tropical night descended, but she heard his step, returning.

"Quite certain there's no danger," he reassured her. "Went back a way."

"Thank you," she said. And added: "For all."

"Betty." The stars twinkled madly. Pulsating waves seemed to vibrate in the air. A moment he continued to stare into the darkness, then again turned. He had not seen how the girl's hand had suddenly closed, and her slender form had swayed. As restlessly he resumed his sentinel's duty, Sonia Turgeinov's last words once more recurred to him. How often had he thought of them that long afternoon, and wondered who was the one the young girl would now shortly be free to turn to? There had been many in the past who had sought her favor. Perhaps the unknown was one of these; or, more likely, one of the newer many that had arisen, no doubt, since, in the gayer larger world of New York, or the continent. Betty Dalrymple's manner at the Russian woman's words indicated that the latter had - how Mr. Heatherbloom could not imagine - hit upon a great kernel of truth. Again, in fancy, he saw on her cheek that swift flush of warm blood. Lucky, thrice lucky, the man who had caused it! Softly Mr. Heatherbloom moved nearer.

Was she sleeping? He, himself, felt too fagged to sleep. Like Psyche, in the glade, she was covered all with starlight. He ventured closer, bent over; the widely opened eyes looked suddenly into his.

"The woman told me you had nothing to do with it - that plot of hers and the prince," she said slowly. "I know now why you were on the boat, and - all the rest - what it meant for me, your being there."

"You know, then" - embarrassed - "the awful mess I made of it all -"

"You dared a great deal," she said softly.

"And came an awful cropper!"

She did not answer directly. "At first Francois was most reluctant to risk going with me," she went on. "I thought it odd, at the time, he should change so suddenly, become so brave. Now I understand, at least, a little - in a general way. I have been over-quick to think evil of you, ever since we met again. Perhaps, in the past, too" - slowly - "I have been -"

"Betty!" he cried uneasily, and seemed about once more to move away, when -

"Don't go," she said. "I'll not talk if you command me not to. You've been the master to-day, you know," with subtle accent.

"Have I?" His voice showed evidence of distress. "I didn't really mean - it was necessary," he ended firmly.

"Of course it was," said the girl. Her accent conveyed no note of displeasure. Profile-wise he saw her face now - the young moon beyond. "Don't think I'm blaming you. I'm not quite so hard, perhaps, as I once was." Mr. Heatherbloom stood back a little farther in the shadow. "Maybe, my poor little standard of judgment -" she stopped. "I have been heedless, heartless, perhaps -"

"You!" he exclaimed. "You!" There was only unfalte-ring adoration in his tone - faith, unchanged and unchangeable.

She spoke with a little catch in her voice: "Oh, I haven't cared. I *did* flirt with the prince; he accused me of that. He was right. What did it matter to me, if I made others suffer? I haven't always had so good a time as I seemed to -" There was a ring of passion in her tone now. "What happened?" she said, turning on him swiftly. "What has happened? I want to know all -"

"You mean about the prince?"

"I know all I want to know about him," scornfully. "I mean" - her slender figure bent toward Mr. Heatherbloom - "you! What has taken place, and why has it? What does it all mean? Don't you understand?"

He drew in his breath slowly.

"Tell me," she said, still tensely poised, her eyes insistent in the shadow of her hair.

"Miss Dalrymple - Betty -" he half stammered.

"I want to know," she repeated. There was an inexorable demand in her gaze. Mr. Heatherbloom straightened. The ordeal? - it must be met - though that box of Pandora were best left unopened. He could not refuse her anything; this she asked of him was not easy to grant, however.

"Where shall I begin?" he said uncertainly. "You know a great deal. There doesn't seem much worth talking about."

"Begin where we left off -"

"Our boy-and-girl engagement? You broke it. Quite right of you!" She stirred slightly. "It was, at best, but a perfunctory business, half arranged by our parents to keep the millions together -"

"You never blamed me a little, then?" she asked.

"I - blame you?" wonderingly. "You were as far from me as a star. What you thought of me, you told me; it was all right - true stuff. Though it sank in like a blade. I was nothing - worse than nothing. A rich man's son! - a commonplace type. A good fellow some called me at Monte Carlo, Paris, elsewhere." He paused. A moment he seemed another personality - that other one. She saw it anew, caught a glimpse of it like a flash on a mirror; then he seemed to relapse farther back into the shadow. "I really don't want to bore you," he said perfunctorily, raising an uncertain hand to the stray; lock on his forehead.

"You aren't - doing that. Go on." Her eyes were full of questions. "After I saw you that last time" - he nodded - "you disappeared. No one ever heard anything of you; again, or knew what had become of you."

"As no one cared," he said with a short laugh, "what did it matter?"

"You were lost to the world - had vanished completely," she went on. "Sometimes I thought - feared you were dead." Her voice changed.

"Feared?" he repeated. "Ah, yes! You did not want me to go out like that."

"No," she said slowly. "Not like that."

He looked at her comprehendingly ; in spite of the

bitter passionate repudiation of him, she had been a little in earnest - had cared, in the least, how he went down.

"Why," he said, with a forced smile, "I didn't think you'd bother to give the matter a thought."

"You had some purpose?" she persisted, studying him. "I see - seem to feel it now. It all - you - were incomprehensible. I mean, when I saw you again that first time, in New York, after so long -"

"It was funny, wasn't it?" he said with rather strained lightness. "The Chariot of Concord - *What's the Matter with Mother?* - the gaping or jibing crowd - then you, going by -"

Her eyelids drooped; he stood now erect and motionless; in spite of the determination to maintain that matter-of-fact pose, visions appeared momentarily in his eyes. The glamour of the instant he had referred to caught him. All he had felt then at the unexpected sight of her - beautiful, far-away - returned to him. She was near now, but still immeasurably distant. He pulled himself together; he hadn't explained very much yet. He was forced to go on; her eyes once more seemed to draw the story from him.

"Yes; I had some purpose in going away like that. The idea came to me at the sanatorium, when I was about 'all in'. They'd managed to keep the drugs and the drink from me, and one day I seemed to wake up and realize I hadn't ever really lived. Just been a tail-ender who had 'gone the pace'. Hadn't even had a beginning. Was it too late to start over again? Probably." His voice came in crisp accents. "But it was a last chance - a feeble one - a straw to the drowning," he laughed. "That sounds absurd to you but I don't know how to explain it better."

"No; it doesn't sound absurd," she said.

"The idea of mine? - how to carry it out? Ways and means were not hard to find. I went to" - he mentioned a name - "an old friend of my father's. He thought I was a fool," bruskly, "but in the end he approved, or seemed to. Anyhow, I persuaded him to take all my bonds, securities and the rest of (for me) cursed stuff. At the end of a certain time, if I wanted back the few millions I hadn't yet run through, he was to give them to me, minus commissions, wage, etc."

"You mean," said the girl, "that was the way you took to go back to the beginning, as you call it?" Her eyes were like stars. "You practically gave away all your money so as to start by yourself."

"How could I start with it?" he asked, with a faint smile. "Don't you see, Betty" - in a momentary eagerness he forgot himself - "there couldn't be any compromising? Besides, it came to me - you will laugh" - she did not laugh - "that some day, somewhere else, if not here, I'd have to make that beginning, to be something myself. Remember that old Hindu fellow with a red turban who sat on your front lawn, beneath the palms, and had the women gathered around him in a kind of hypnotic state? He said something like that - I thought him an old fakir at the time. He used a lot of flowery language, but I guess, boiled down, it meant start at the bottom of the ladder. Build yourself up, the way my father did," with a certain wistful pride. "You remember him?"

FREDERIC STEWART ISHAM

Her head moved. "Fine looking, wasn't he?" rumina-
tively. "He got there with his hands and brains, and
honestly. While I hadn't ever used either. I hope," he
broke off, "all this doesn't sound like preaching."

"No," she said.

An instant his gaze lingered on her. "You're sleepy
now," he spoke suddenly.

"No, I am not. You found it a little hard, at first?"

"A little. When a man is relaxed and the reaction is on
him - " He stopped.

"Tell me - tell me all," she breathed. "Every bit of it,
Harry."

His lips twitched. To hear his almost forgotten name
spoken again by her! A moment he seemed to waver.
Temptation of violet eyes; wonder of the rapt face! Oh,
that he might catch her in his arms, claim her anew;
this time for all time! But again he mastered himself
and went on succinctly, as quickly as possible.
Between the lines, however, the girl might read the
record of struggles which was very real to her. He had
reverted "to the beginning" with poor tools and most
scanty experience. And there was that other fight that
made it a double fight, the fiercer conflict with self.
Hunger, privation, want, which she might divine,
though he did not speak of them, became as lesser
details. She listened enrapt.

"I guess that's about all," he said at last.

She continued to look at him, his features, clear-cut in

the white light. "And you didn't ever really go back - to undo it all?"

"Once I did go back to 'Frisco" - he told her of the relapse with cold candor - "out at heels, and ready to give up. I wanted the millions. They were gone."

"You mean, lost?"

"Yes; he had speculated; was dead. Poor fellow!"

"You say that? And you have never tried to get any of the money back?"

"Fortunately, he died bankrupt," said Mr. Heatherbloom calmly.

"And you failed to show the world he was a - thief?" Something in the word seared her.

"What was the use? He left a wife and children. Besides, he really served me by what the world would call robbing me. I *had* to continue at the beginning. It was the foot of the ladder, all right," he added.

Her face showed no answering gaiety. "You are going to amount to a great deal some day," she said. "I think very few of us in this world find ourselves," she added slowly.

"Perhaps some don't have to hunt so hard as others," observed Mr. Heatherbloom.

"Don't they?" Her lips wore an odd little smile.

He threw back his shoulders. "Good night, now. You

are very tired, I know."

She put out her hand. He took it - how soft and small and cold! The seconds were throbbing hours; he couldn't release it, at once. The little fingers grew warmer - warmer in his palm - their very pulsations seemed throbbing with his. Suddenly he dropped her hand.

"Good night," he said quickly.

He remembered he was nothing to her - that they would soon part for ever.

"Good night," she answered softly.

Then, silence.

CHAPTER XXIV

AN EXPLANATION

Morn came. They had heard or seen nothing of the prince and his men. Mr. Heatherbloom walked back for a cold plunge in a stream that had whispered not far from their camping spot throughout the night. He and Betty Dalrymple breakfasted together on an old log; it wasn't much of a meal - a few crackers and crumbs that were left - but neither appeared to mind the meagerness of the fare. With much gaiety (the dawn seemed to have brought with it a special *allegrezza* of its own) she insisted upon a fair and equitable division of their scanty store, even to the apportioning of the crumbs into two equal piles. Then, prodigal-handed for a castaway who knew not where her next meal might come from, she tossed a bit or two to the birds, and was rewarded by a song.

All this seemed very wonderful to Mr. Heatherbloom; there had never before been such a breakfast; compared to it, the *dejeuner a la fourchette* of a Durand or a Foyot was as starvation fare. It was surprising how beautiful the dark places of the night before looked now; daylight metamorphosed the spot into a sylvan fairyland. Mr. Heatherbloom could have lingered there indefinitely. The soft moss wooed him, somewhat aweary with world contact; she filled his eyes. The faint shadowy lines beneath hers which he had noted at the dawn had now vanished; the same sun-god that ordered the forest flowers to lift their gay heads commanded the rosebuds to unfold their bright petals on her cheeks. Her lips were as red berries; the cobwebs, behind, alight with sunshine, gleamed no more than the tossed golden hair. She had striven as best she might with the last, not entirely to her own satisfaction but completely to Mr. Heatherbloom's. His untutored masculine sense rather gloried in the unconventionally of a superfluous tangle or two; he found her most charming with a few rents in her gown from branch or brier. They seemed to establish a new bond of camaraderie, to make blithe appeal to his nomadic soul. It was as if fate had directed her footsteps until they had touched and lingered on the outer circle of his vagabondage. Both seemed to have forgotten all about his excellency.

"Rested?" queried Mr. Heatherbloom.

"Quite," she answered. There was no trace of weariness in her voice. "And you?"

"Ditto," he laughed. Then, more gravely, "You see, I fell asleep while watching," he confessed.

"I'm glad."

"You'd make a lenient commanding officer. Shall we go on?"

"Where?"

"I don't exactly know," he confessed.

"That's lovely." Then, tentatively, "It's nice here."

"Fine," he assented. There was no hardness in the violet eyes as they rested on him. He did not pause to analyze the miracle; he only accepted it. A moment he yielded to the temptation of the lotus-eater and continued to luxuriate in the lap of Arcadia. Then he bestirred himself uneasily; it was not sufficient just to breathe in the golden gladness of the moment. "Yes; it's fine," he repeated, "only you see -"

"Of course!" she said with a little sigh, and rose. "*I* see you are going to be very domineering, the way you were yesterday."

"I? Domineering?"

"Weren't you?" she demanded, looking at him from beneath long lashes.

"I'm sure I didn't intend -" He stopped for she was laughing at him. They went on and her mood continued to puzzle him. Never had he seen her so blithe, so gay. She waved her hand back at the woodland spot. "Good-by," she said.

Then they came upon the little town suddenly - so suddenly that both appeared bewildered. Only a hillock had separated them from the sight of it the night before. They looked and looked. It lay beneath an upward sweep of land, in a cosy indenture of a great circle that swept far around and away, fringed with cocoanut trees. Small wisps or corkscrews of smoke defiled the blue of the sky; a wharf, with a steamer at the end, obtruded abruptly upon the curve of the shore. Mr. Heatherbloom regarded the boat - a link from

Arcadia to the mundane world. He should have been glad but he didn't seem overwhelmed at the sight; he stood very still. He hardly felt her hand on his sleeve; the girl's eyes were full of sparkles.

"What luck!" he said at length, his voice low and somewhat more formal.

"Isn't it?" she answered. And drawing in her breath - "I can scarcely, believe it."

"It's there all right." He spoke slowly. "Come." And they went down. A colored worker in the fields stared at them, but Betty nodded gaily, and asked what town it was and the name of the island. He told them, growing wonderment in his gaze. How could they be here and not know that; where had they come from? To him they were as mysterious as two visitants from Mars. Regardless of the effect they produced on the dusky toiler they walked on. The island proved to be larger than they had thought and commercially important. They had, the day before, but crossed a neck of it.

Soon now they reached the verge of the town and stood on its main artery of traffic; the cobblestone pavement resounded with the rattling of carts and rough native vehicles. At a curb stood a dilapidated public conveyance to which was attached a horse of harmoniously antique aspect. Miss Dalrymple got in and Mr. Heatherbloom took his place at her side.

"The cable office," said the girl briefly, whereupon a lad of mixed ancestry began to whack energetically the protuberant ribs of the drowsy steed. It woke him and they clattered down the narrow way. Mr.

Heatherbloom leaned back, his gaze straight ahead, but Betty Dalrymple looked around with interest at the people of divers shades and hues, and, for the most part, in costumes of varying degrees of picturesque originality. After having narrowly escaped running over a small proportion of the juvenile colored population overflowing from odd little shops and houses, they reached the transportable zinc shed that served as a cable office. Here Miss Dalrymple indited rapidly a most voluminous message, paid the clerk in a businesslike manner, and, unmindful of his amazed expression as he read what she had written, tranquilly re-entered the carriage.

"Miss Van Rolsen will be relieved when she gets that," observed Mr. Heatherbloom mechanically. "It'll be a happy moment for her," meditatively.

"And won't she be gladder still when she sees us?" answered the girl gaily.

The use of the plural slightly disconcerted Mr. Heatherbloom for the moment, but he dismissed it as an inadvertence. "Where now?" he asked.

"Where do you think?" with dancing eyes. "Shopping, of course. Fortunately I drew plenty of money before starting for California."

An hour or so later Mr. Heatherbloom sat with parcels in his arms and bundles galore around him. He accepted the situation gracefully; indeed, displayed an almost tender solicitude for those especial packages she herself handed him.

"What next ? " She had at length exhausted the

somewhat limited resources of the thoroughfare.

"Drive to the best hotel," was her command. She laughed at the picture he made, or at something in her own thoughts. She had unconsciously assumed toward him a manner in the least proprietary, but if he noticed he did not resent it. They went faster; her voice was a low thread of music running through an accompaniment of crashing dissonances. She wore a hat now - the best she could find. He considered it most "fetching", but her thrilling derision overwhelmed his expression of opinion. Though the way was so rough that they were occasionally thrown rather violently one against another, they arrived in high spirits at their destination, Mr. Heatherbloom having performed the commendable feat of preserving intact the parcels and bundles en route. In the "best hotel" they were given two rooms overlooking a courtyard redolent with orchids. The girl nodded a brief farewell to him from the threshold of her room.

"In about an hour, please, come back."

He did, brushed up and with shoes shined, as presentable as possible. She wore the same gown, but the sundry rents were mended and there had occurred other changes he could divine rather than define. He brought her information - not agreeable, he said. He was very sorry, but the next boat for the United States would not call at the island for a fortnight. He expected her to show dismay, but she received the news with commendable fortitude, if not resignation.

"I can cable aunt every day - so there can be no cause for worry - and she will only be the more pleased when we actually do arrive."

Again the plural! And once more that prophetic picture which included Mr. Heatherbloom within the pale of the venerable and austere Miss Van Rolsen's jubilation. He looked embarrassed but said nothing. During the hour of his exclusion from Miss Dalrymple's company he had sallied forth on a small but necessary financial errand of his own. Francois had placed in the basket of biscuits a revolver, and this latter Mr. Heatherbloom, rightfully construing it as his own personal property in lieu of the weapon his excellency had deprived him of, had exchanged for a bit of cardboard and a greenback. The last named, reinforced by the small amount Mr. Heatherbloom had left upon reaching the *Nevski* and of which the prince had not deprived him, would relieve his necessities for the moment. After that? Well, he would take up the problem presently; he had no time for it now. This day, at least, should be consecrated to Betty Dalrymple.

He had an inkling that on the morrow he would see less of her; the girl's story would get around. The American consul would call and tender his services. The governor, too, Sir Charles Somebody, whose palatial residence looked down on the town from the side of the hill, might be expected to become officially and paternally interested. The little cable office, despite rules and regulations, could not long retain its prodigious secret; moreover Mr. Heatherbloom, in an absent-minded moment, had inscribed Miss Dalrymple's name on the register, or visitors' book. He recalled how the eyes of the old mammy, the proprietress, had fairly rolled with curiosity. No; he would not be permitted long to have her to himself, he ruminated; better make the most of his opportunity now. Besides, his present monetary position forbade his presence for more than a day or two at the "best hotel"; its rates were for him distinctly prohibitive. The exigencies of financial differences would soon separate them; she could draw on Miss Van Rolsen for thousands; he had but five dollars and twelve cents - or was it thirteen? - to his name.

He kept these reflections, however, to himself and continued to bask in the sunshine of a fool's paradise. They rode, walked and explored. They went to the fruit and the flower market. He bought her a great bunch of flowers, and she not only took it but wore it. For a time he stepped on air; his flowers constituted a fine splash of color on the girl's gown. Her heart beat beneath them; the thought was as wine.

"Shall we?" They had partaken of tea (or nectar) in a small shop, and now she paused before that most modern manifestation of a restless civilization, a begilded, over-ornamented nickelodeon. "Think of finding one of them way off here! Just as at home!"

"More extraordinary your wanting to go in!" he laughed.

"Why not? It will be an experience."

They entered; the place was half filled and they took seats toward the back. There were films, and songs of the usual character; it was very gay. Gurgles of merriment from Creoles and darkies were heard on all sides. They, too, yielded freely, gladly to its infection. Happy Creoles! happy darkies! happy Betty Dalrymple and Horatio Heatherbloom - heiress and outcast! There is a democracy in laughter; yon darky smiled at Miss Dalrymple, while Mr. Heatherbloom laughed with her, with them, and the world. For was she not near, right there by his side? To Mr. Heatherbloom the tinsel palace had become a temple of felicity and wonder. Suddenly he started and his face changed.

"The Great Diamond Robbery," one of the films, was in progress, and there, depicted on the canvas, amid many figures, he saw himself, the most pronounced in that realistic group. And Betty Dalrymple saw the semblance of him, also, for she gave a slight gasp and sat more erect. In the moving picture he was running away from a crowd.

"Shall - shall we go?" The face of the flesh-and-blood Mr. Heatherbloom was very red; he looked toward the door.

She did not answer; her eyes continued bent straight before her, and she saw the whole quick scene of the drama unfolded. Then the street became cleared, the fleeing figure had turned a corner as an automobile, not engaged for the performance, came around it and went by. A big car - her own - she was in it. She caught, like a flash on the canvas, a glimpse of herself looking around; then the scene came to an end. Betty Dalrymple laughed - a little hysterically.

"Oh," she said. "Oh, oh!"

He became, if possible, redder.

"Oh," she repeated. Then, "Why" - with eyes full of mingled tragedy and comedy - "did you not explain it all that day, when -"

Of course she knew even as she spoke why he could not, or would not.

"You had cause to think so many things," he murmured.

"But that! How - how strange! I saw you, and -"

He laughed. "And the manager told me I was a 'rotten bad' actor! Those were his words; not very elegant. But I believed him, until now -"

"Say something harsh and hard to me," she whispered, almost fiercely. "I deserve it."

The violet eyes were passionate. "Betty!" he exclaimed wonderingly.

"Do you call that harsh?" she demanded mockingly. "You - you should be cross with me - scold me - punish me -"

"Well," he said calmly, "you haven't believed *that*, lately, anyhow."

"No; I just set it aside as something incomprehensible, not to be thought of, or to be considered any more. I believed in you, with all my soul, since last night - a good deal before that, yes, yes! - in my innermost heart! You believe me, don't you?"

He answered, he hardly knew what. Some one was singing *Put on Your Old Gray Bonnet*. Her shoulder touched his arm and lingered there. "Oh, my dear!" she was saying to herself. The pianist banged; the vocalist bawled, while Mr. Heatherbloom sat in ecstasy.

CHAPTER XXV

GAIETIES

They took her away the next day. The governor - Sir Charles Somebody - had heard of her and came and claimed her. His lady - portly, majestic - arrived with him. Their carriage was the finest on the island and their horses were the best. The coachman and footman were covered with the most approved paraphernalia and always constituted an unending source of wonder and admiration for the natives. The latter gathered in front of the best hotel on this occasion; they did not quite know what was taking place, but the sight of the big carriage there drew them about like flies.

Mr. Heatherbloom did not linger to speculate or to survey. He had seen but not spoken to Miss Dalrymple that morning; she had smiled at him across space, behind orchids. A moment or two he had sat dreaming how fine it would be to live for ever in such a courtyard, with Betty Dalrymple's face on the other side, then the hubbub below disturbed and dispelled his reflections. He went down to investigate and to retreat. Sir Charles and his lady were in the hall; they seemed to charge the entire hostelry with their presence. Mr. Heatherbloom walked contemplatively out and down the street.

His mind, with a little encouragement, would have flitted back to courtyards and orchids, but he forced it along less fanciful lines. Mundane considerations were imperative and courtyards were a luxury of the rich. He calculated that, after paying his bill at the best hotel, he wouldn't have much more than half a dollar, or two English shillings, left. The situation demanded calm practical reflection; he strove to bestow upon it the necessary measure of orderly thinking. Yesterday, with its nickelodeon, or temple of wonder, was yesterday; to-day, with its problems, was to-day. He had lingered in the happy valley, or kingdom of Micomicon, but the carriage was before the door - the golden chariot had come to bear away the beautiful princess.

Mr. Heatherbloom asked for employment at the wharf and got it. The supercargo of the boat, loading there, had been indulging, not wisely but too well, in "green swizzles", an insidious drink of the country, and, when last seen was oblivious to the world. A red-haired mate, with superfluous utterance, informed the applicant he could come that afternoon and temporarily essay the delinquent one's duties, checking up the bags of merchandise and bananas the natives were bringing aboard, and otherwise making himself useful. Mr. Heatherbloom tendered his thanks and departed.

He wandered aimlessly for a while, but the charm of the town had vanished; he gazed with no interest upon quaint bits most attractive yesterday, and stolidly regarded now those happy faces he had liked so much but a short time before. He shook himself; this would not do; but the work would soon cure him of vain imaginings.

He returned to the hotel and settled with the landlady. Betty Dalrymple was gone. Of course, there could be no denying Sir Charles and his lady; one of the young girl's place and position in the world could not, with reason or good grace, refuse the governor's hospitality. Mr. Heatherbloom was hardly a suitable chaperon. But she had left a hasty and altogether charming note for him which he read the last few moments he spent in the courtyard room. "Come soon;" that was the substance of it. What more could mortal have asked? Mr. Heatherbloom gazed at an empty window where he had last seen her (had they been there only twenty-four hours?), then he took a bit of painting on ivory from his pocket and wrapped the message around it. Before noon he had engaged cheap but neat lodgings at the home of an old negro woman.

Several days passed. After waiting in vain for him to call at the governor's mansion, Betty Dalrymple drove herself to the hotel; here she learned that he had gone without leaving an address; a message from Sir Charles for Mr. Heatherbloom, formally offering to put the latter up at government house, had not been delivered. Mr. Heatherbloom had failed to call for his mail.

"Really, my dear, such solicitude!" murmured the governor's wife, when Miss Dalrymple came out of the hotel. "An ordinary secret-service man, too."

"Oh, no; not an ordinary one," said the girl a little confusedly. She had not taken the liberty of speaking of Mr. Heatherbloom's private affairs to her august hosts. His true name, or his story, were his to reveal when or where he saw fit. In taking her into his confidence he had sealed her lips until such time as she

FREDERIC STEWART ISHAM

had his permission to speak.

"Well, don't worry about the man," observed the elder lady rather loftily. "There has been a big reward offered, of course, and he'll appear in due time to claim it."

"He'll not," began Betty Dalrymple indignantly, and stopped.

She had been obliged to explain in some way Mr. Heatherbloom's presence, and the subterfuge he had himself employed toward her on the *Nevski* had been the only one that occurred to her. A brave secret-service officer who had aided her - that's what Mr. Heatherbloom was to the governor and his better half. Hence the distinct formality of Sir Charles' note to Mr. Heatherbloom, indited at Miss Dalrymple's special request and somewhat against the good baronet's own secret judgment. A police agent may be valiant as a lion, but he is not a gentleman.

Something of this axiomatic truth the excellent hosts strove to instill by means, more or less subtle, in the mind of their young guest; but she clung with odd tenacity to her own ingenuous point of view. Whereupon Sir Charles figuratively shrugged. Reprehensible democracy of the new world! She, with the perversity of American womankind, actually spoke of, and, no doubt, desired to treat the fellow as an equal.

She found him one morning, a day or two later. She came down to the wharf, alone, and on foot. He held a note-book and pencil, but that he had not been above lending physical assistance, on occasion, to the natives bearing bags and other merchandise, was evident from his hands which were grimy as a stevedore's. His shirt was open at the throat, and his face, too, bore marks of toil. Betty Dalrymple stepped impetuously toward him; she looked as fresh as a flower, and held out a hand gloved in immaculate white.

"Dare I?" he laughed.

"If you don't!" Her eyes dared him not to take it.

He looked at the hand, such a delicate thing, and seemed still in the least uncertain; then his fingers closed on it.

"You see I managed to find you," she said. "Who is that man who stares so?"

"That," answered Mr. Heatherbloom smiling, "is my boss."

"Well," she observed, "I don't like his face."

"Some of the darkies he's knocked down share, I believe, your opinion," he laughed. "Excuse me a moment." And Mr. Heatherbloom stepped to the dumfounded person in question, handed him the note-book and pencil, with a request to keep tab for a moment, and then returned to the girl. "Now, I'm at your command," he said with a smile.

"Suppose we take a walk?" she suggested. "We can talk better if we do."

A moment Mr. Heatherbloom wavered. "Sorry," he then said, "but I've promised to stick by the job. You see the old tub sails to-morrow for South America and it'll be a task to get her loaded before night. Some of the hands, as well as the supercargo, have been bowled over by fire-water."

"I see." There was a strained look about her lips. Before them heavily laden negroes and a few sailors passed and repassed. The burly red-headed mate often looked at her; amazement and curiosity were depicted on his features; he almost forgot the duties Mr. Heatherbloom had, for a brief interval, thrust upon him. Betty Dalrymple, however, had ceased to observe him; he, the others, no longer existed for her. She saw only Mr. Heatherbloom now; what he said, she knew he meant; she realized with an odd thrill of mingled admiration and pain that even she could not cause him to change his mind. He would "stick to his job", because he had said he would.

"I'm interrupting, I fear," she said, a feeling of strange humility sweeping over her. "When is your day's work done?"

"About six, I expect."

"The governor gives a ball for me to-night," she said.

"Excellent. All the elite of the port will be there, and," with slow meditative accent, "I can imagine how you'll look!"

"Can you?" she asked, bending somewhat nearer.

"Yes." His gaze was straight ahead.

The white glove stole toward the black hand. "Why don't you come?"

"I?" He stared.

"Yes; the governor has sent you an invitation. He thinks you a secret-service officer."

Mr. Heatherbloom continued to look at her; then he glanced toward the boat. Suddenly his hand closed; he hardly realized the white glove was in it. "I'll do it, Betty," he exclaimed. "That is, if I can. And - there may be a way. Yes; there will be."

"You mean, you may be able to rent them?" With a sparkle in her glance.

"Exactly," he answered gaily, recklessly.

Both laughed. Then her expression changed; she suppressed an exclamation, but gently withdrew her hand.

"How many dances will you give me, Betty?" He had not even noticed that he had hurt her; his voice was low and eager.

"Ask and see," she said merrily, and went. But outside the shed, she stretched her crushed fingers; he was very strong; he had spoiled a new pair of gloves; she did not, however, seem greatly to mind. As for Mr. Heatherbloom, for the balance of the day he plunged into his task with the energy of an Antaeus.

*   *   *   *   *

Sir Charles regarded rather curiously that night one of his guests who arrived late. Mr. Heatherbloom's evening garments were not a Poole fit, and his white gloves, though white enough, had obviously been used and cleaned often. But the host observed, also, that Mr. Heatherbloom held himself well, said just the right thing to the hostess, and moved through the assemblage with quite the proper poise. He didn't look bored, neither did he appear overimpressed by the almost palatial elegance of the ball-room. He even managed to suppress any outward signs of elation at the sight of Miss Dalrymple with whom he had but the opportunity for a word or two, at first. Naturally the center of attraction, the young girl found herself forced to dance often. He, too, whirled around with others, just whom, he did not know; he dipped into Terpsichorean gaiety to escape the dowager's inquisition regarding that haphazard flight from the *Nevski* and other details he did not wish to converse about. But his turn came with Betty at last, and sooner than he had reason to expect.

"Ours is the next?" she said, passing him.

Was it? He had ventured to write his name thrice on her card, but neither of the dances he had claimed was the next.

"I put your name down for this one myself," she confessed to him a few moments later. "Do you mind?"

Did he? The evening wore away but too soon; he held her to him a little while, only over-quickly to be obliged to yield her to another. And now, after a third period of waiting, the time came for their last dance. He went for it as soon as the number preceding was over; he wanted, not only to miss none of it, but he hungered to snatch all the prelude he could. The conventional-looking young personage she had been

dancing with regarded the approaching Mr. Heatherbloom rather resentfully, but he moved straight as an
arrow for her. At once she stepped toward him, and he
soon found himself walking with her across the smooth
shining floor, on into the great conservatory. Here
were soft shadows and wondrous perfumes. Mr.
Heatherbloom breathed deeply.

"But a few days more, and we're en route for home." It
was the girl who spoke first - lightly, gaily - though
there was a thrill in her tones.

He started and did not answer at once. "That will be
great, won't it?" His voice, too, was light, but it did not
seem so spontaneously glad as her own.

"You *are* pleased, aren't you?" she said suddenly.

"Pleased? Of course!"

A brief period of inexplicable constraint! He looked at
one of her hands resting on the edge of a great vase - at
a flower she held in her fingers.

"May I?" he said, and just touched it.

"Of course!" she laughed. "A modest request, after all
you've done for me!"

Her fingers placed it in the rented coat.

"There!" she murmured in a matter-of-fact tone,
stepping back.

His face, turned to the light, appeared paler; his eyes
looked studiously beyond her.

"It will be jolly on the steamer, won't it?" she went on.

"Jolly? Oh, yes," he assented, with false enthusiasm, when a black and white apparition appeared before them, no less a person than Sir Charles.

The governor, as the bearer of particular news, had been looking for her. Mr. Heatherbloom hardly appreciated the preamble or the importance of what followed. Sir Charles imparted a bit of confidential information they were not to breathe to any one until he had verified the particulars. Word had just been brought to him that the *Nevski* had gone on a reef near a neighboring island and was a total wreck. A passing steamer had stood by, taken off the prince and his crew and landed them. Still Mr. Heatherbloom but vaguely heard; he felt little interest at the moment in his excellency or his boat. Betty Dalrymple's face, however, showed less indifference to this startling intelligence.

"The *Nevski* a wreck?" she murmured.

"It must all seem like an evil dream to you now," Mr. Heatherbloom spoke absently. "Your having ever been on her!"

"Not all an evil one," she answered. They stood again on the ball-room floor. "Much good has come from it. I no longer hate the prince. I only blame myself a great deal for many things -"

He seemed to hear only her first words. "'Good come from it?' I don't understand."

"But for the *Nevski*, and what happened to me, I should

have gone on thinking, as I did, about you."

"And - would that have made such a difference?" quickly.

She raised her eyes. "What do you think?"

"Betty!"

The music had begun. He who had heretofore danced perfectly, now guided wildly.

"Take care!" she whispered.

But discretion seemed to have left him; he spoke he knew not what - wild mad words that would not be suppressed. They came in contact with another couple and were brought to an abrupt stop. Flaming poppies shone on her cheeks; her eyes were brightly beaming. But she laughed and they went on. He swept her out of the crowded ball-room now, on to the broad veranda where a few other couples also moved in the starlight. On her curved lips a smile rested; it seemed to draw his head lower.

"Betty, do you mean it?" Again the words were wrested from him, would come. "What your eyes said just now?"

She lifted them again, gladly, freely - not only that -

"Yes; I mean it - mean it," said her lips. "Of course! Foolish boy! I have long meant it -"

"Long?" he cried.

"You heard what the Russian woman said -"

"About there being some one? Then it was -"

"Guess." The sweet laughing lips were close; his swept them passionately. He found the answer; the world seemed to go round.

But later, that night, there was no joy on Mr. Heatherbloom's face. In his room in the old negro woman's house, he indited a letter. It was brought to Betty Dalrymple the next morning as the early sunshine entered her chamber overlooking the governor's park.

"Darling: Forgive me. I am sailing at dawn on the old tub, for South America -"

Here the note fell from the girl's hand. Long she looked out of the window. Then she went back to the bit of paper, took it and held it against her breast before she again read. She seemed to know now what would be in it; the strange depression that had come over her after he had left last night was accounted for. Of course, he would not go back to New York with her; he would, or could, accept nothing, in the way she wished, from her or her aunt. It was necessary for him still to be Mr. Heatherbloom; he had not yet "found himself" fully; the beginning he had spoken of was only begun. The influential friends of his father in the financial world had become impossible aids; he had to continue as he had planned, to go his own way, and his, alone. It would have been easy for him, as his father's son and the prospective nephew of the influential Miss Van Rolsen, to have obtained one of those large salaried positions, or "sinecures", with little to do. But that would be only beginning at the end once more.

Again she essayed to read. The letter would have been a little incomprehensible to any one except herself, but she understood. There were three "darlings"; inexcusable tautology! She kissed them all, but she kissed oftenest the end: "You will forgive me for forgetting myself - God knows I didn't intend to - and you will wait; have faith? It is much to ask - too much; but if you will, I think my father's son and he whom you have honored by caring for, may yet prove a little worthy -"

The words brought a sob to her throat; she threw herself back on the bed. "A little?" she cried, still holding the note tight in her hand. But after a spell of weeping, once more she got up and looked out of the window. The sunshine was very bright, the birds sang to her. Did she take heart a little? A great wave of sadness bowed her down, but courage, too, began to revive in her.

"Have faith?" She looked up at the sky; she would do as he asked - unto the grave, if need be. Then, very quietly, she dressed and went down-stairs.

EPILOGUE

It is very gay at the Hermitage, in Moscow, just after Easter, and so it was natural that Sonia Turgeinov should have been there on a certain bright afternoon some three years later. The theater, at which she once more appeared, was closed for the afternoon, and at this season following Holy Week and fasting, fashionables and others were wont to congregate in the spacious cafe and grounds, where a superb orchestra discourses classical or dashing selections. The musicians played now an American air.

"Some one at a table out there on the balcony sent a request by the head waiter for it," said a member of Sonia Turgeinov's party - a Parisian artist, not long in Moscow.

"An American, no doubt," she answered absently, sipping her wine. The three years had treated her kindly; the few outward changes could be superficially enumerated: A little more embonpoint; a tendency toward a slight drooping at the corners of the mobile lips, and moments when the shadows seemed to stay rather longer in the deep eyes.

"That style of music should appeal to you, Madam," observed the Frenchman. "You who have been among those favored artists to visit the land of the free. Did you have to play in a tent, and were you literally showered with gold?"

"Both," she laughed. "It is a land of many surprises."

"I have heard *es ist alles* 'the almighty dollar'," said a musician from Berlin, one of the gay company.

"Exaggeration, *mein Herr!*" she retorted, with a wave of the hand. "It is also a *komischer romantischer* land." For a moment she seemed thinking.

"Isn't that his excellency, Prince Boris Strogareff?" inquired abruptly a young man with a beyond-the-Volga physiognomy.

She started. "The prince?" An odd look came into her eyes. "Do you believe in telepathic waves, Monsieur?" she said gaily to the Frenchman.

"Not to any great extent, Madam. *Mais pourquoi?"*

"Nothing. But I don't see this prince you speak of."

"He has disappeared now," replied her countryman, a fellow-player recently come from Odessa. "It is his first dip again into the gaieties of the world. For several years," with the proud accents of one able to impart information concerning an important personage, "he has been living in seclusion on his vast estates near the Caspian Sea - ruling a kingdom greater than many a European principality. But have you never met the prince?" To Sonia Turgeinov. "He used to be a patron of the arts, according to report, before the sad accident that befell him."

"I think," observed Sonia Turgeinov, with brows bent as if striving to recollect, "I did meet him once. But a poor actress is forced to meet so many princes and nobles, nowadays," she laughed, "that -"

"True! Only one would not easily forget the prince, the handsomest man in Asia."

She yawned slightly.

"What was this 'sad accident' you were speaking of, *mein Herr*? observed the German, with a mind trained to conversational continuity.

"The prince was cruising somewhere and his yacht was wrecked," said the young Roscius from Odessa. "A number of the crew were drowned; his excellency, when picked up, was unconscious. A blow on the head from a falling timber, or from being dashed on the rocks, I'm not sure which. At any rate, for a long time his life was despaired of, but he recovered and is as strong and sound as ever. Only, there is a strange sequel; or not so strange," reflectively, "since cases of its kind are common. The injury was on his head, as I remarked, and his mind became -"

"Affected, Monsieur?" said the Frenchman. "You mean this great noble of the steppe is no longer right, mentally?"

"He is one of the keenest satraps in Asia, Monsieur. His brain is as alert as ever, only he has suffered a complete loss of memory."

Sonia Turgeinov's interest was of a distinctly artificial nature; she tapped on the floor with her foot; then abruptly arose. "Shan't we go into the garden for our coffee?" she said. "It is close here."

They got up and walked out. As they did so they passed a couple at one of the tables on the balcony and a slight exclamation fell from Sonia Turgeinov's lips. For an instant she exhibited real interest, then hastening down the steps, she selected a place some distance aside. A great bunch of flowers was in the center of the table and she moved her chair behind them.

"You see some one you know, *gnaedige* Madam?" asked the observant Teuton.

"A great many people," she answered.

"There's that American over there who asked for the Yankee piece of music," said the Frenchman, with eyes on the two people Sonia Turgeinov had started at sight of, a moment before. "*Mon Dieu!* What charm! What beauty!"

"*Der Herr Amerikaner?*" blurted the surprised Berliner.

"No - *diable!* His *belle* companion!"

"Where?" said Sonia Turgeinov, well knowing. A face that her table companion regarded, she, too, saw beyond the flowers. The afternoon sunshine touched the golden hair of her she looked at; the violet eyes shone with delight upon bizarre details: of the scene - the waiters in blouses resembling street "white wings" in American cities, the coachmen outside, big as balloons in their quilted cloaks.

"*Der Herr Amerikaner* has the passionate eyes of an admirer, a devout lover," murmured the sentimental musician from Berlin.

"Or an American husband!" said Roscius from Odessa.

"Sometimes!" added the Frenchman cynically.

"I haf met him," observed the *Herr Musikaner*, "at the hotel. We haf talked together, once or twice. He has been in South America - Argentine, *ich glaube* - and has made a fortune there. And madam, his wife, and he are making a grand tour of the world. Their wedding trip, I believe.*Sie kommt von einer der ersten Familien* - the Dalrymples. *Der Herr Direktor* of the Russicher-Chinese bank told me. He cashes the drafts - *Her Gott - nicht kleine!*"

These prosaic details the Frenchman, pictorially occupied, hardly, heard. "*Mon Dieu*! What a *chapeau*!" he sighed. "No wonder he looks enchanted at that wonderful creation of the Rue de la Paix."

"He seems quite an exception to some husbands in that respect!" remarked the Berliner in deep gutturals.

Sonia Turgeinov lighted a cigarette and blew the smoke at the flowers. There was a resentful cynicism in the act; she leaned back with greater abandon in her chair. "After all, the unities have been observed," she said with an odd laugh.

"What unities?" asked Roscius, becoming keen as a young hound on the scent, at the sound of the trite phrase.

"Oh, I was thinking of a play." Stretching more comfortably. Suddenly her cigarette waved; behind the flowers, her eyes dilated. Prince Boris Strogareff was coming down the steps; he passed the American couple they had been talking about and looked at them. A light of involuntary admiration shone from his gaze, but there was no recognition in it - only the instinctive tribute that a man of the world and a gallant Russian is ever prone to pay at the sight of an unusually charming member of the other sex. Then, once more impassive - a striking handsome figure - he moved leisurely down and out of the gardens. The couple, engrossed at the time in a conversation of some intimate nature or in each other, had not even seen or noticed the august nobleman.

Sonia Turgeinov drew harder on the cigarette; a laugh welled from her throat. "Oh, I wouldn't have missed it for worlds!" she said.

Young Roscius with the Tartar eyes stared at her. She threw away the smoking cylinder.

"I'm off!"

"Why -"

"Has not the curtain descended?" enigmatically.

"I don't see any curtain," said the Frenchman.

"No? But it's there." At the gate, however, once more she paused - to listen, to laugh.

"*Was jetzt?*" asked the mystified Berliner.

FREDERIC STEWART ISHAM

She only shrugged.

The orchestra, having played a few conventional selections after *Dixie*, had now plunged into *Marching through Georgia*.

As Sonia Turgeinov disappeared through the gate, the golden head surmounted by the "wonderful *chapeau*", bent toward the clean-cut, strong-looking face of the young man on the other side of the small table.

"It's awfully extravagant of you, Harry, - twenty roubles, a tip for those musicians. But it makes it seem like home, doesn't it?"

"Yes, darling," he answered.

Choose from Thousands of 1stWorldLibrary Classics By

Adolphus WilliamWard
Aesop
Agatha Christie
Alexander Aaronsohn
Alexander Kielland
Alexandre Dumas
Alfred Gatty
Alfred Ollivant
Alice Duer Miller
Alice Turner Curtis
Alice Dunbar
Ambrose Bierce
Amelia E. Barr
Andrew Lang
Andrew McFarland Davis
Anna Sewell
Annie Besant
Annie Hamilton Donnell
Annie Payson Call
Anton Chekhov
Arnold Bennett
Arthur Conan Doyle
Arthur Ransome
Atticus
B. M. Bower
Basil King
Bayard Taylor
Ben Macomber
Booth Tarkington
Bram Stoker
C. Collodi
C. E. Orr
C. M. Ingleby
Carolyn Wells
Catherine Parr Traill
Charles A. Eastman
Charles Dickens
Charles Dudley Warner
Charles Farrar Browne
Charles Ives
Charles Kingsley
Charles Lathrop Pack
Charles Whibley
Charles Willing Beale
Charlotte M. Braeme
Charlotte M.Yonge
Clair W. Hayes
Clarence Day Jr.
Clarence E. Mulford

Clemence Housman
Confucius
Cornelis DeWitt Wilcox
Cyril Burleigh
D. H. Lawrence
Daniel Defoe
David Garnett
Don Carlos Janes
Donald Keyhole
Dorothy Kilner
Dougan Clark
E. Nesbit
E.P.Roe
E. Phillips Oppenheim
Edgar Allan Poe
Edgar Rice Burroughs
Edith Wharton
Edward J. O'Biren
John Cournos
Edwin L. Arnold
Eleanor Atkins
Elizabeth Cleghorn
Gaskell
Elizabeth Von Arnim
Ellem Key
Emily Dickinson
Erasmus W. Jones
Ernie Howard Pie
Ethel Turner
Ethel Watts Mumford
Eugenie Foa
Eugene Wood
Evelyn Everett-Green
Everard Cotes
F. J. Cross
Federick Austin Ogg
Ferdinand Ossendowski
Francis Bacon
Francis Darwin
Frances Hodgson Burnett
Frank Gee Patchin
Frank Harris
Frank Jewett Mather
Frank L. Packard
Frederick Trevor Hill
Frederick Winslow Taylor
Friedrich Kerst
Friedrich Nietzsche
Fyodor Dostoyevsky

Gabrielle E. Jackson
Garrett P. Serviss
Gaston Leroux
George Ade
Geroge Bernard Shaw
George Ebers
George Eliot
George MacDonald
George Orwell
George Tucker
George W. Cable
George Wharton James
Gertrude Atherton
Grace E. King
Grant Allen
Guillermo A. Sherwell
Gulielma Zollinger
Gustav Flaubert
H. A. Cody
H. B. Irving
H. G. Wells
H. H. Munro
H. Irving Hancock
H. Rider Haggard
H. W. C. Davis
Hamilton Wright Mabie
Hans Christian Andersen
Harold Avery
Harold McGrath
Harriet Beecher Stowe
Harry Houidini
Helent Hunt Jackson
Helen Nicolay
Hendy David Thoreau
Henrik Ibsen
Henry Adams
Henry Ford
Henry Frost
Henry James
Henry Jones Ford
Henry Seton Merriman
Henry Wadsworth
Longfellow
Henry W Longfellow
Herbert A. Giles
Herbert N. Casson
Herman Hesse
Homer
Honore De Balzac

Horace Walpole
Horatio Alger, Jr.
Howard Pyle
Howard R. Garis
Hugh Lofting
Hugh Walpole
Humphry Ward
Ian Maclaren
Israel Abrahams
J.G.Austin
J. Henri Fabre
J. M. Barrie
J. Macdonald Oxley
J. S. Knowles
J. Storer Clouston
Jack London
Jacob Abbott
James Allen
James Lane Allen
James Andrews
James Baldwin
James DeMille
James Joyce
James Oliver Curwood
James Oppenheim
James Otis
Jane Austen
Jens Peter Jacobsen
Jerome K. Jerome
John Burroughs
John F. Kennedy
John Gay
John Glasworthy
John Habberton
John Joy Bell
John Milton
John Philip Sousa
Jonathan Swift
Joseph Carey
Joseph Conrad
Joseph Jacobs
Julian Hawthrone
Julies Vernes
Justin Huntly McCarthy
Kakuzo Okakura
Kenneth Grahame
Kate Langley Bosher
L. A. Abbot
L. T. Meade
L. Frank Baum
Laura Lee Hope

Laurence Housman
Leo Tolstoy
Leonid Andreyev
Lewis Carroll
Lilian Bell
Lloyd Osbourne
Louis Tracy
Louisa May Alcott
Lucy Fitch Perkins
Lucy Maud Montgomery
Lydia Miller Middleton
Lyndon Orr
M. H. Adams
Margaret E. Sangster
Margaret Vandercook
Maria Edgeworth
Maria Thompson Daviess
Mariano Azuela
Marion Polk Angellotti
Mark Overton
Mark Twain
Mary Austin
Mary Cole
Mary Rowlandson
Mary Wollstonecraft
Shelley
Max Beerbohm
Myra Kelly
Nathaniel Hawthrone
O. F. Walton
Oscar Wilde
Owen Johnson
P.G.Wodehouse
Paul and Mable Thorn
Paul G. Tomlinson
Paul Severing
Peter B. Kyne
Plato
R. Derby Holmes
R. L. Stevenson
Rabindranath Tagore
Rahul Alvares
Ralph Waldo Emmerson
Rene Descartes
Rex E. Beach
Richard Harding Davis
Richard Jefferies
Robert Barr
Robert Frost
Robert Gordon Anderson
Robert L. Drake

Robert Lansing
Robert Michael Ballantyne
Robert W. Chambers
Rosa Nouchette Carey
Ross Kay
Rudyard Kipling
Samuel B. Allison
Samuel Hopkins Adams
Sarah Bernhardt
Selma Lagerlof
Sherwood Anderson
Sigmund Freud
Standish O'Grady
Stanley Weyman
Stella Benson
Stephen Crane
Stewart Edward White
Stijn Streuvels
Swami Abhedananda
Swami Parmananda
T. S. Ackland
The Princess Der Ling
Thomas A. Janvier
Thomas A Kempis
Thomas Anderton
Thomas Bailey Aldrich
Thomas Bulfinch
Thomas De Quincey
Thomas H. Huxley
Thomas Hardy
Thomas More
Thornton W. Burgess
U. S. Grant
Valentine Williams
Victor Appleton
Virginia Woolf
Walter Scott
Washington Irving
Wilbur Lawton
Wilkie Collins
Willa Cather
Willard F. Baker
William Makepeace
Thackeray
William W. Walter
Winston Churchill
Yei Theodora Ozaki
Young E. Allison
Zane Grey